STARTUP FIANCÉ

SHILPA MUDIGANTI

The characters and events in this book are fictitious. Any similarity to real persons, living or dead, places, or events is coincidental and not intended by the author.

If you purchase this book without a cover you should be aware that this book may have been stolen property and reported as "unsold and destroyed" to the publisher. In such case the author has not received any payment for this "stripped book."

Startup Fiancé

Copyright © 2018 Shilpa Mudiganti

All rights reserved.

Edited By Jessica Martinez

Cover art By BookishGals

This book, or parts thereof, may not be reproduced in any form without permission. The copying, scanning, uploading, and distribution of this book via the internet or via any other means without the permission of the publisher is illegal and punishable by law. Please purchase only authorized electronic or print editions, and do not participate in or encourage piracy of copyrighted materials. Your support of the author's rights is appreciated.

AUTHOR'S NOTE

Dear Reader,

I am glad you picked up my book to read.

The main characters of this story are of Indian subcontinent origin. To keep the authenticity of their voice, I have included some cultural references with the actual *Hindi* words and language usage. Below is a quick reference for you.

Beta translates to *son*.

Sherbet in Indian subcontinent is actually a fruit-flavored, cool, and refreshing drink.

In casual conversations, there is a tendency to call the name first and the relationship after. For example, it's *John uncle* instead of *uncle John*. When you see this in the story, please know it is not an editing miss but a deliberate attempt to keep the voice authentic.

If you have any more questions, or curious to know more about the cultural references in the book, please do contact me by emailing me here.

Thank you again,
Shilpa Mudiganti

1

———

ARAV

Ifs and buts don't exist in the world of business. If you want to win the cut-throat competition, you have to go all in and get bloodied. And yet, I found myself contemplating an "if". What if I fired Tom Pattinson? What would I have to lose? I could find a new marketing head. I thought it over as he hunched over his computer and droned on about the dismal figures. I stood facing away from Tom and toward Times Square, hands in my pockets, forcing myself not to punch something.

I am Arav Shetty, a thirty-two-year-old self-made billionaire. I started TechNotes eight years ago, and I have never looked back. And yet, at that moment, I found myself wondering if all my effort had fallen short.

"Launch updates?" I asked.

"15,000 sales yesterday, Arav. And we're already at 8,000 today. So, we're on track to meeting the sales goal." I could hear him swallow. The chair creaked a bit as he shifted in his seat.

"Website traffic?"

"105,000 since this morning. Better than yesterday."

"Just by 0.01%" Tom swallowed again. I looked away from the window just long enough to notice beads of sweat rolling down his scraggly cheek as he focused on providing an acceptable answer. He started typing notes furiously in an effort to avoid looking at me.

Tall, dark and ruthless - that's what TIME magazine had written about me. I was known for many things in the world of technology, but I was particularly famous for my competitive nature and complete intolerance for incompetence.

"I am going to check with our developers to see if the website's tracking code has an error," Tom said finally, closing his laptop. He hastened to get to the door but stopped short when he heard me call his name.

"Check with Sandra Meyer to see if the website links in our products are broken. There is nothing wrong with the website codes. I checked them this morning. You should have, too." Tom averted his eyes as soon as they met mine. I was sure my eyes reflected nothing but annoyance. Annoyance at him. "And ask Greg to reassign you to the testing team."

I turned back to the window, effectively dismissing Tom. The moment the soft click of the door registered, an involuntary sigh escaped me. Hands on my hips, I stared at the flashing billboard in the middle of Times Square. The fifteen-second advertisement of TechNotes flashed, and a little crowd pointed at the massive screen in awe. It cost me a fortune to get those fifteen seconds in the middle of such a famous world landmark, but boy, was I proud of the result. Yet, I feared failure, feared all that I built in the last eight years would turn to dust with this product launch.

Competition was fierce, and it only got more intense when Note Nirvana launched the year before. Within six months,

Note Nirvana had swiped 2 percent of TechNotes users. The founder and CEO of the company, Nisha Jain, was a tough cookie, but I relished the competition. I was ready for the fight and had turned around their latest app features in a record three months' time. I was proud of what we accomplished, until this morning. Our spectacular launch and sales started dipping the moment Note Nirvana even *announced* their latest set of features. The features weren't even in the product, and yet, users were willing to wait. I squeezed the back of my neck, relieving some of the tension that was building up. What wouldn't I give to have such a loyal customer base!

Now Tom seemed to be having a mid-life crisis right in the middle of the launch! If there was anything that I hated more than product failures, it was the incompetent people behind those failures. But I wasn't about to allow failure in TechNotes.

I rolled up the sleeves of my dress shirt high enough to hide the Armani logo, and bent over the laptop on my desk to check on the website again. The massiveness of my oak desk always annoyed me, but appearances had to be kept. At least that's what Ryan Penn, my best friend and company CFO thought. Website traffic was high - but could be higher. My fingers itched to rewrite some of the code, but my engineering lead would bite my head off. I had done enough meddling in the process, thanks to the years of coding I put into the product. I gripped the desk, pent frustration threatening to blow. I needed to get out of the office and clear my head.

I had just put on my suit jacket when my phone rang. It was my uncle. Mild panic fluttered in my chest. I had been living with Krish uncle since I moved to United States fourteen years ago. He never called during the day unless its urgent. I pressed the speaker button on the phone, shaking off the tension.

"Yes, Uncle. Everything ok?"

"Absolutely, *beta*. Are you busy? I have something important to discuss." I looked at my watch and frowned. I pulled my shirt sleeve, straightening my suit, and took the phone off speaker.

"Sure," I said, "Is it Seema auntie's diabetes? I swear I will buy out the bakery and close it if she doesn't stop visiting there every day."

Uncle's hearty chuckle eased my tension. "I would love to see *that* showdown someday, but that's not it. Your aunty is healthy and continues to aggravate my blood pressure." he paused. "I called you to talk about a marriage proposal that came in today."

"Don't you think it's a bit early to plan for a second marriage when Aunty is still around?" I smirked, knowing my words would irritate him. I couldn't believe that he'd call me just to tell me about another gold digger marriage proposal that would tie me down. Knowing this was going to take time, I walked to the tanned leather couch at the other end of my office and flopped down on its rich, cool smoothness.

"It's never too early to think about a second wife. But, jokes aside, I wouldn't call if I didn't think this girl could be it." I had to roll my eyes at that.

"You said the same thing the last time around, and she turned out to be a professional con."

"And I ensured she won't be out from behind bars - for at least five years." His voice was low and rumbling, and I felt a pang of guilt. After all, it was my fault too that I never checked out Tanya's background.

"Believe me, this girl is not a con. In fact, you both have a lot in common. She graduated from Yale, like you, and heads a company now." My ears perked up. Intelligence was a turn-on, definitely, but what about the huge ego that came with success? Hell, sometimes I was so difficult that I wouldn't marry myself. But, guilt was clawing its way up my throat.

"That's good...good. So...email me her details. I will get in touch." Wincing, I thumped my fist on my forehead. When would I learn the art of saying no to my uncle? My uncle's glee was nauseating and thankfully, he ended the call soon after. I flopped back on the couch and sighed. Getting fixed up was not in my plan this week. This week was about our product launch and watching my app's subscriber base climb while Note Nirvana's dissolved bit by bit.

I rubbed my jaw. My five o'clock shadow felt like sandpaper on my fingers. Yeah, I needed a shave before I met this wonder-woman. But, the shave and the meeting could wait a week. I needed to fix my company first. A renewed resolve fueled me off the couch. I decided to pay a visit to the engineering floor and take things in my own hands.. I took one quick glance at my computer, only to find my uncle's matchmaking email had arrived. But I never got the chance to actually read it that day.

THE SLAM of my car door did nothing to soothe the furious mood I was in. I stood outside my car, breathing heavily. *This couldn't be real. Had to be a nightmare.* Oh, who was I kidding! Note Nirvana was featured in TechWorld's e-magazine, the most popular and respected ezine amongst techies. Not only was the review glowing, the reviewer had the gall to take a dig at my company, and say we needed to make way for the new *queen* of note-making apps, an apparent reference to Nisha Jain.

Like an ominous sign, the garage light ticker stopped and the light went off, bathing me in darkness. I closed my eyes, willing myself not to yell at the garage light like a lunatic. Light seeped from under the door to the house and I took confident steps towards it, my feet intimately aware of every bump and hairline crack on the path.

As I entered my living space, I dropped my jacket on the black leather couch. I went straight to the kitchen and reached for the Johnny Walker. The sound of the trickling liquid into the crystal glass soothed me right away. I took a quick swig and winced. The rich blend burst in my mouth and the warmth slid down my throat, bringing an instant release to my tense mood. The improvement was minor, but it helped me think clearly. The smoky aftertaste urged me to pour another, but I wasn't a drunkard. Images of my drunken father flashed before me. Fear of turning into him was the best possible deterrent. But that night, I didn't want to think about Dad.

I had walked out - no, *marched* out of my office the moment I heard the news. Now, I pulled up the article on my phone and read it all over again. The shock of it was milder than before, but nevertheless, the sting didn't lessen.

Nisha's headshot accompanied the article. With my jaw set, I stared at her long enough to memorize every curve of her face. The first thing I noticed were her bow-like lips, pink and set with a smile. The smile was pleasant - the kind New Yorkers regularly give to strangers. Her sharp nose and high cheekbones proved her lineage of rich forefathers. I bristled at that. *Another "founder" with a silver spoon and no shortage of funds, talking of startup struggles.* And yet, I kept looking back at her mesmerizing light brown eyes. Her eyes were at odds with everything else in the photo. They held life, pure and genuine, and they gave her face a look of innocence. She was a beauty, even though admitting so felt like swallowing glass. Unfortunately for me, her smart brain was determined to ruin my company. I locked the phone and let out a tired sigh.

I pushed myself off the couch and unbuttoned my shirt as I strode towards the bedroom. My brain was fried and ready to give in to a deep slumber. I hit the pillow face first with nothing on but my boxers, cherishing the cool sheets on my hot skin. I turned around, relishing the soft pressure on my scalp as I ran my hands through my hair. My thoughts dragged me back to the renewed pressure at work. My company was all I cared about. My business's success represented everything that I was - which was *not* my father. Not a drunkard who almost killed his wife with his addiction. Not a failed businessman. I was a success story and I built that success through countless hours of nothing but hard work.

I just couldn't get Nisha Jain out of my mind.

I knew the App industry was risky and highly competitive. I wasn't naive enough to think there would be no competitors who would threaten my company's number one ranking. What I didn't imagine was being thrown off with no notice. Note Nirvana burst onto the market just a few months before and it had already amassed a million users - close to thirty percent of my company's user base. Users were moving away, slowly but surely and I had to stop the bleed.

I tossed to the side and grabbed my phone off the side table. I started playing around with the Note Nirvana app on my phone. I had grudgingly installed it couple of months back as "competitor research." I should have done it sooner.

Lips pursed, I tried ignoring the effectiveness of the soothing colors, and how easy it was to move my notebooks around. I shut my eyes, hoping the renewed frustration would just pass. *I have to talk to my UX designers about the colors on our app.* We would probably also need new sets of user-friendly features, not to mention the fact that we had to top the new features Nisha announced this week. Her announcement had caused a ruckus in the market.

But, all of this meant more investment in app features that might not pan out. Nisha Jain had one-upped us since she burst onto the scene. *Speaking of investments...*an idea began forming in my mind. The excitement of such a possibility gave me goosebumps. My fingers raced on the keypad as they keyed in Note Nirvana's company details. I quickly scanned through rows of company statistics, feeding my hunger to know more. I found nothing in the statistics to derail my idea. For the first time since I read that unnerving article, I felt positive. I quickly typed an email to Ryan, asking him to get more details about Note Nirvana. Then I closed my eyes for sleep. I was relieved that I finally had a reason to smile that night - but Nisha Jain's eyes were already there, lulling me into dreamless slumber.

THE CONSISTENT TAPPING was getting to me. I looked up from my laptop at Ryan, who was sitting across from me, eyes glued to his laptop. He had one hand on his cheek, and the other hand held the offending pen, which was tapping away on the desk. Ryan didn't seem the least bit bothered by the noise. He probably didn't hear it. Once he was in the "number zone," he was lost to the world. Apparently, that was when his brilliance shone and he came out with his mind-blowing insights. That was the only reason I swallowed the mind-numbing, erratic sound. But it had been close to an hour now, with no reprieve. I dragged my fingers through my hair, trying to tune out the tapping, when it suddenly went a notch higher. *Did he just start tapping his right foot too?* I stood abruptly. The desk hit my thigh, but I didn't even wince. The pain was actually a good two-second distraction from the noise.

"I am going for coffee," I announced.

"Wait up, I'll come too." The guy could listen, after all. "What?" Ryan was probably a couple of inches taller than my six feet, but right now, I would have no trouble punching the smirk off his face.

"Why are you so noisy when you work?" Hands on my hips, I was spoiling for a fight after all of the noise pollution in the room.

"What noise, man? I was having the time of my life dissecting Nirvana's finances. I think you are on to something here." Tilting his head sideways, he winked. I didn't fight my smile as relief rushed through me. We might have an actual chance to contain the competition.

"So what next?" I asked as I opened the door of my office. We decided to walk to the coffee shop across the street. The August air was warm, and I was glad I was in my linen casual than the usual stuffy suit.

"I will have my team run the numbers and get a valuation in couple -" A bike dashed right in front of us and we jumped back onto the sidewalk. "Hey, *moron*! What is your *problem*?!" Ryan yelled after him. "Did you see that cyclist? I could have died, man. Embarrassing!" He rubbed his chest, still furious at the unnamed cyclist who had just given us a rigid middle finger. Watching Ryan return the gesture with both hands was comical. I slapped his back to redirect his attention.

"You are alive, bro. Move on." He shook his head. I led us across the street this time, keeping an eye on Ryan in case he decided to run and take on the cyclist. After we were safely on the other side of the street, I picked up the topic again. "So when will you get me the report?"

"Oh yeah, probably a couple of days. Hey, why don't you go meet this chick and see what's up?" We stood waiting in line to order at the coffee shop. That made me think. Yes, I could probably meet Nisha and try to come up with some sort of a mutually beneficial deal. But...

"I don't want to look desperate. Nisha is a new player. I need to have the upper hand in negotiations." His blue eyes clouded with confusion.

"Why would I ask you to meet Nisha without my numbers? I meant the girl that Krish talked to you about."

"I suppose my uncle called you." It was not a surprise - just a mild irritation. It didn't matter that I was thirty-two now. To my uncle, I was still the sixteen-year old kid he needed to keep an eye on. To the point where he would even snoop around my friends and talk them into making me do things that he would never ask me to do directly.

Ryan nodded. Taking a sip from his coffee, he said, "We chatted a while about golf before he snuck this cool chick who seems to have it all into the conversation. When I told him you never said anything to me about her, he made me promise that I would talk to you. So here I am, Arav, telling you to go meet this chick." He fished out his phone. "Let me text Krish, now that my job is done."

We took a seat by the window. Legs stretched under the table, I stared out at people walking by on the sidewalk while Ryan texted my uncle. For a moment, I wasn't thinking about business. My thoughts turned to that nameless "chick," as Ryan called her. Or, "the one" as my uncle called her. She could be my wife - the one I was going to share my life with, the good, bad and the ugly. Could I really "arrange" this relationship and come out of it lucky? And was I really ready for it, considering I had completely forgotten about this discussion with my uncle? I had gone a full day and a half without giving it a second thought. Would this girl be okay with me forgetting to call her or bring her presents? My crash-bound train of thought was interrupted by Ryan.

"How does this go, anyway? Are you going to go and interview her or something? Are you allowed to ask her if she is a virgin?" Ryan's mischievous smile was not lost on me. He had this weird idea that arranged marriage is an interview, where the groom gets to ask the bride a few questions, and depending on the answers, she gets the esteemed job of being his wife.

That was how marriages were arranged in the past. Neither the groom nor the bride had much say in the matter. Families met and the decision was made, with just a picture of the groom or bride to hold onto before the wedding. If they were lucky, the bride and groom were allowed to be in the same room when the elders of the family talked about their compatibility. But that was the way of the past. It didn't work like that anymore.

Nowadays, not only did the bride and groom get to meet each other, but the parents only played the role of matchmaker. The actual decision rested with the couple, who usually met for a couple of dates without the family hovering around. But, no matter how many times I explained this to Ryan, he still stuck to his original theory.

"Why don't you come with me? Maybe, you can do the

interview and I can watch." I said as I sipped my dark coffee. The coffee break was already putting me in a good mood.

"No man, then she'll insist on marrying me. I like non-virgins. Sets the expectations way lower." As if he needed to set any expectations. His picture-perfect face alone had launched a few cat fights around him.

"Honestly, I don't have time for this right now. Let's fix the Nirvana situation first and then I will think about it."

"Whatever works," he said, raising his cup. "To business before pleasure."

The next hour was spent sorting out our next board meeting and the budget for the rest of the year. But, the thought of marriage kept tugging me away from the task at hand.

I had never had any problem maintaining my relationships in the past. Yet, the past couple of years had been insanely busy, with little or no time for a woman in my life. A couple of dates here and there were all I could fit in. Some dates were better than others, but none got me hooked, and I was fine with that. But a committed relationship and marriage?

My family thought I was ready to take the leap. But, I didn't think I was. The idea of marriage did nothing for me. If anything, memories of my abusive dad were all I could conjure up. Would I turn into him? My mom had sent me away to her brother in United States to save me from my dad, fearing I would be his next target. But where would my wife send our son?

My mood soured, and I stayed back at the coffee shop after Ryan left. I scrolled through the images on my phone for the last picture of my mother and I before she sent me here. I was fourteen then. Draped in a light orange saree, she stood behind me with her hands on my shoulders. We both gazed at the camera, my face bright with a smile. I stared at the image of my mom, with a rare, shy smile on her face. I remembered that when I had turned back to look up at her, after the flash of the camera pretty much blinded us, I was in awe, because she looked so beautiful.

I closed my eyes, still feeling her soft palms on my cheeks as she smiled wider for me. That smile would help me sail through the tough times in my life. If she could live with that excuse of a man for my sake, nothing could stop me from doing her proud. But she was no longer with me - no more letters full of concern, no more choppy video chats. Only memories. I wished she could see me now and tell me whether I was like my father. Honestly, I wished she would vehemently deny any trace of my father in me. I just wished she were here.

2

———

NISHA

The screen flickered once, then twice, forcing Calista Wein, our head of product development, to pause her presentation. All eight of us looked up together at the overhead projector, frustration testing the best among us. This was the third time in a two-hour marketing workshop that the projector decided to ruin the moment for us. The remote wasn't working, either. We all turned to Jake Long in unison. He was the only marketing analyst there, and, at six-foot-three, he was the tallest guy in the room. He groaned and straightened to his full height. With his arm outstretched, it was child's play for him to switch on the projector. The projector came to life again with a lazy humming sound, its light illuminating the whiteboard. A graph, pointing north, showed up on the screen. A slow smile formed on my lips as I savored another victory this week in the war with TechNotes. Calista, looking confident in her clean-cut professional suit, continued with her analysis.

"We have seen a three percent growth in our user base since last week. That's a growth of 1.5% from the previous week. And, I expect this week to be an even better showing after our new feature announcement. The response has been extremely encouraging," she said.

"Speaking of the new features," I said to Calista, "how's the product development coming along?" Calista's stubby fingers punched more letters into her iPad before she pointed to the presentation screen.

"Here's me chatting about a note with our Nirvana developer," she declared, to some enthusiastic wooting. We had been so excited about adding chat and collaboration to our repertoire, and it was gratifying to see it all in action.

"Always with the dramatics." I said, smiling as I nodded at the iPad in her hand. She passed it to me, glee stretching her chubby cheeks to the point of cuteness. Calista was short, huge and extremely cuddly, and she had the best brain around. I had pretty much thanked heaven every day since she accepted my meager offer four months before. Apparently, she was a sucker for sleepless nights and impossible goals.

As I swiped the screen and explored the work in progress on our product, my shot nerves from the morning began to feel soothed again. We had started the day with an investor meeting, which went much more roughly than I had anticipated. I had not expected Note Nirvana to go for series two funding so soon, but we had pretty much bootstrapped the first round. Our first couple of investors were small - not that I cared. I had poured in my life savings in the company along with them. I guess I was naive to think that just because the app was doing well now, it would be easy to convince these new, bigger investors to invest in my company. But, they didn't say no, and they had some leading questions, which I liked. There was hope, as our CFO Mark Young said. Now, experiencing our new features first hand, I was *sure* there was hope.

I was listening to the animated chatter between Calista and the team on how to get the word out when my phone buzzed with a text.

Unknown number: Hey Nisha, this is Arav, from TechNotes. Great job with Note Nirvana. Would love to catch up sometime soon. Take care. Arav.

My heart raced a million miles a minute, and I could feel my cheeks heat up. I re-read the text, forehead scrunched, wondering if it was real. Arav Shetty, CEO of our arch-rival, who famously rose to success with brilliance and hard work, was texting *me*. My lips curled up, a happy song in my heart. If he was texting me, Note Nirvana must be kicking some butt!

Nisha: Hi Arav. Thanks. Catching up sounds good. Let me know what day and time suits you. I can get my PA to set it up.

Three dots danced nimbly on my screen immediately. He was typing a reply.

Arav: I am on 59th St. right now, meeting someone. How about we meet in an hour at the coffee shop below your office? If you are available, that is.

I bit my lower lip, debating. Unscheduled meetings with rivals were never a good idea and Arav, with his track record of stunning wins among his competitors, was the last person I should be having coffee with. And yet, I was greedy. I wanted to meet my biggest competitor and find out who I was dealing with, in an informal and neutral space. With no pressure to close a deal or pitch my company. He proposed coffee, and I agreed. Simple. I checked my watch - 3:00 would be a perfect time for my own coffee fix.

Nisha: See you at three, then. Text once you are here.
Arav: See you soon.

I clicked my phone off and excused myself from the meeting. I strode towards my office through the engineering department. Images of our app adorned most of the 29-inch desktop monitors, while the developers sat at their computers tapping out code. The engineers were the real deal. Without their magic code, Note Nirvana would have been just another note-taking app. I quickened my steps, swearing not to jeopardize their work and their future when I met Arav in an hour.

I spotted Mark, a pen in his mouth, seemingly lost in a paper he had in his hand. With his hair splayed on the sides and balding in the center, Mark looked older than his forty-two years. It seemed to me that working with numbers all day might age anyone, but I never dared bring it up to him. Mark's short temper was well-known even before I poached him from his former employer, but I didn't care as long as he could do the numbers right. And there, I had no complaints. I stopped at his side and tapped his shoulder. He jumped slightly, his ears reddening immediately.

"Next time, just call me, will you? You scared the living daylights out of me."

"Yes sir!" I mock saluted him. "I need you, urgently. Got a sec for me?" Lips pursed, he looked back at the paper in hand.

"Can it wait a bit? I can be there in 10 minutes."

"Sure. Just come right in whenever you're ready." I said. I left him alone with his beloved number-filled paper. I had to prepare for Arav's meeting. Even though we were competing big-time with TechNotes, none of us had taken any interest in finding out personal details about Arav Shetty. If he had reached out to me on my cell phone, when I had not even shared my number with him, he had definitely done his homework already. I could not go unprepared. I quickly typed his name in my phone browser and thousands of results filled up the screen. Most were about TechNotes. I scrolled down, searching for something more personal that would give me a feel for who he was. Head down, I opened the door to my office - and bumped straight into someone. My phone slipped, making a soft thud on the carpet floor.

"Ugh." I bent down to pick up the phone. "Sorry I didn't se... Nik? What are you doing here?" I straightened, adjusting my knee length, grey suit dress. Nik, a.k.a. Nikhil Mehra, my ex-fiancé, was smiling at me, hands extended, apparently expecting me to fall in his arms. His polo shirt and beige pants fit his GQ model image perfectly, but his optimism was misplaced. I stepped around him to my side of the desk, waiting for an answer.

"I came to see you. To see how you are doing." He took the seat across me, the sting of his rejected embrace clear on his face. He quickly replaced his disappointment with a perfect smile, graced by his perfectly aligned teeth.

"I am good. Busy as usual," I said, hands clasped on the table. I needed him to leave as soon as possible.

"Of course. Don't we all know how busy you are with this hobby of yours." He rolled his eyes. "I cannot wait for the day when you're done with all of this. Then we can get married with no distractions." He lounged in the chair, bouncing it back gently.

"Nik, there won't be any marriage between us. I am not coming back to you."

"You are. This whole circus won't take long to crash. I heard you are looking for funds now. Are things that bad?" I almost wanted to punch his smug face. This was why I broke off our engagement. He always thought this venture of mine was a *hobby*, something I did to keep myself busy. Initially, his attitude hurt - the guilt trips he gave me when I couldn't make it to every swanky party he had to go to, and the way he shamed me for my absence in front of my family. He took every opportunity to embarrass me about this passion of mine. To him, I was the chosen arm candy for the heir of Mehra Enterprises. The marriage alliance between our families was formed when I was sixteen. It had been ten years now, and supposedly it was only a matter of time before we tied the knot. Maybe that was the plan once, but not anymore.

"Our finances are none of your business, Nik. Can we talk later? I have an important meeting to prepare for." I powered up my desktop and tried not to dwell on his disappointed sigh.

" If you want money, you can always ask me, OK? You don't have to go to all these investors. My money is your money and-"

"Enough Nik! You forget that I am the daughter of Kamlesh Jain, the third richest Indian American. If I needed money, I already have it. I do not have to ask you for it." I shook with anger. I stood abruptly, rage pouring off me. "And I am not your fiancé anymore. Get out and-"

"Sorry, is this a bad time?" Mark peeked into the room, his eyes darting between me and Nik . I shook my head and waved at him to come inside, unable to trust my voice. I sighed and looked up at Nik. His gaze was unreadable, just like it was on the billboards that adorned half of New York City.

"I will be there at Sean's wedding next Saturday. So, I'll see you there," he said, as he walked to the door. I wanted to tell him not to count on it, but it would be no different than talking to the wall. I slumped in to my chair and rubbed my eyes. I didn't take Nik to be a romantic, especially since our engagement was a perfectly managed event coordinated by his secretary. But, he turned out to be more invested in our relationship than I ever imagined.

"I didn't realize resolving lover-boy problems was in my job description. Do you really expect me to fix *that*?" Mark crossed his legs and tapped his fingers on his knee. I groaned, rubbing my face in frustration.

"I would hope not, Mark!" I opened my desk drawer, pulled out a hair tie and quickly pulled my hair into a knot. "Arav Shetty texted me a few minutes back. We are having coffee in... twenty-four minutes," I said, checking my watch. I winced, realizing how much time had been wasted squabbling with Nik. Mark's eyebrows shot to his forehead.

"You're kidding. How did this happen? What does he want from you?" He sat forward, pulling his pen out from behind his ear as he tore a page from the spare notepad on my desk. Always ready.

"He texted me. and I don't know what he wants." That's what I am going to go find out. What do you know about Arav?" He massaged his bald patch and adjusted his thick glasses.

"Smart. Hawkish. I am not sure you should meet him at on such short notice." I had expected his response, but I was ready to take my chances. I wanted to know what he had in mind when he thought to reach out to me. I knew curiosity killed the cat but, well, I was no ordinary cat.

"Anything more useful? Should I worry about getting poisoned?" I asked, trying to lighten the mood. He chuckled. He scribbled something on the paper and pushed it towards me. I stared at the eight-figure number on it.

"If he turns on his magic and starts talking about buying Note Nirvana, don't even blink until he mentions a number above that." He sat back in the chair, hands cupping the back of his head. The smug smile on his face was encouraging. I had had an idea of why Arav wanted to meet me, but I hadn't dared think about it. Mark confirmed my suspicions. Arav wanted to buy out his competition.

My face mirrored his lopsided smile. "Yes, boss."

I ARRIVED FIVE MINUTES EARLY. Observing Arav's mannerisms when he arrived would give me a psychological head start, and I intended to use the advantage. Three o'clock was usually a busy time at this particular coffee shop – smack inbetween lunch and the end of the business day, and the perfect time for waking up doozy lunch brains with a shot of caffeine.

I tried to navigate my way around the long, curved line which stretched out to the door. I had begun to doubt whether we would get a table here at this hour. When I finally emerged from behind the order line, I looked around for an empty table. My heart sank as I noticed there were no tables available. I almost missed the table with only one patron, who was looking right at me. My heart thudded in my chest as I recognized his attractive face. Arav Shetty was already here, and he was holding a table for us. He had gotten the head start that I meant to have. His light brown eyes met mine and I could swear my pumping heart would pitter-patter out of my chest. I smiled tentatively, and he stood up in recognition. He was tall - around six feet - uncommon for an Indian man. I took quick steps towards him, hoping I looked as confident as he did.

"Hey Nisha, so good to meet you," he said, with a firm shake of my hand. He had a deep voice - the kind that they always use to narrate stories about legendary heroes. I noticed how his blue suit clung to his arms in a perfect fit, and how his cream-colored shirt was open at the base of the neck. Every bit of his clothing was custom-tailored to perfection. His attire was so perfect that the absence of tie stood out. He probably was trying to make this meeting look more casual than it was.

Power rippled around him. I could almost touch the tension in the air as our hands met. I resisted the urge to rub the hand that had just touched him. The remnants of the shock still tingled my palm.

"Nice to meet you too. I was surprised to receive your text," I said. His eyes twinkled at that.

"Surprise is good. Always good. Do you want to order something first?" He looked slightly distracted. I figured he was buying time, and I decided to go with it. I wasn't prepared for the force his personality brought to the table, and a shot of dark coffee would help quite a bit, in fact. I rattled off my order. He nodded and rose to join the long line. I tried not to notice his confident gait, and the way he stood in the line with his hands in his pant pockets. He didn't bring out his phone to pass his time like almost everyone else in line. In the crowd of bent heads, his was looking straight ahead, with no fear of meeting someone's eye.

I mentally went back over all the conversations I imagined I would have with Arav Shetty. The man I saw in front of me was a force of nature, and I need to be on guard and protect my business. Just then, he turned to look at me and gave me a smile. Lips pressed, I smiled back. His eyes held the same twinkle that got my heart racing the first time. I steeled myself. This coffee meeting had just become more challenging than I ever thought it would be.

3
____

ARAV

The barista was openly checking me out by the time it was my turn to order. She gave me a slow smile, her eyes fluttering more than usual. I smiled back and told her what I wanted.

"Will that be all?" I nodded while she waited for the receipt to print out. I stood trying to dislodge Nisha Jain's high voltage smile from my mind when I noticed the barista giving me an odd look. She peeled the receipt from the printer and handed it over to me. Before I could take it, she pulled back and said, "You are someone famous. I swear I saw you on a magazine cover recently." That would have been the High-Tech magazine.

"I get that a lot. But, I am not famous." I said. I kept my tone casual, but she looked disappointed. She gave me my receipt and I moved to the other end to get our coffees. I looked back at Nisha, who was focused on her phone. That worked for me, because I was able to get a good look at her.

Thick, shiny dark hair fell softly on her shoulders. Every feature on her face was etched with care and her body was perfection. It was no surprise that heads turned when she entered the coffee shop. But I didn't expect her to affect me this way. When our hands met, merely focusing on talking sense felt like an impossible task. Her beauty, combined with her incredible presence, was phenomenal - but I was not supposed to not lose it like this. This was a business meeting, and yet, my heart sped up every time she smiled at me. *She has turned me into a bloody teenager.*

I walked back to her with our coffees, determined to keep the eager teenager at bay. She gave me a smile as I handed her the coffee. I barely managed to not spill it all over her. I was Arav fricking Shetty and I needed a *distraction* from checking out my business rival.

"Thanks for the coffee." She took a quick sip and I purposely looked away from her lips to focus on the busy New York streets outside. "This is a busy time at the coffee shop." I nodded in agreement. I should have picked a quieter time, but this was my only free spot for the day. I had to talk to her as soon as I could, before Note Nirvana dropped another product release bomb on us. The reminder of how dangerous her company was to mine was like a shot of caffeine to my brain. The haze she created cleared out and I felt more in control.

"So, tell me more about the success that is Nisha." I sipped my coffee, watching her every movement. She was clearly taken aback. She opened her mouth to answer and thought better of it. I gave her an encouraging smile. She had already exposed a vulnerability that I was determined to use. She wasn't used to personal questions. Or, maybe this question in particular.

"What do you want to know?" she asked, her slender fingers firm around her cup.

"Anything that you would like to share. I have an unhealthy obsession for knowing how it all started. That one spark. That first struggle. It's quite fascinating." It was, in fact, so fascinating that I spent every spare minute reading up on startup stories. Incredible stories of bravery and looking life right in the eye when it's bullying you.

Her fingers relaxed on her coffee cup. She bit her lower lip, a fond smile on her face.

"I developed some apps when I was at Yale. I always knew I would do something in this field. One day, I realized while there were thousands of note-taking apps out there, they were all...pretty unusable." She stopped midway, realizing her slip. "TechNotes was the only half decent one around," she added with a mischievous smile.

"Thank you." I bowed my head in mock reverence. Her smile was disarming but dimmed as soon as it appeared. She cleared her throat and took a quick sip.

"Well, so, I decided to try building a note-taking app the way I thought it should be. I showed it to few friends, and they loved it. I decided to take the plunge." Her journey was quite similar to that of others I had read about, except not many of them had the advantage that she had. and hence, their companies never saw the light of the day. Not everyone's father was among the richest Americans.

"And here you are, with over fifty employees in less than a year. Quite impressive." I wished I could keep the bite out of the words but it irritated me to no end that some people could have it so easy. Her smile dimmed further. She sat back, hands crossed.

"You don't really sound impressed, Mr. Shetty," she said, smirking. I leaned forward, resting my elbows on the table.

"Next, you'll say you started the company in a garage."

"That's exactly what I did. I started Note Nirvana in my dad's garage. I had no mo-"

"You mean, a closed parking lot in your Dad's

Manhattan mansion? I imagine Mr. Jain owns over a dozen cars. Quite a struggle story, Ms. Jain." I watched as color rose to her cheeks. Lips pursed, her shoulders rose and fell as her anger built up.

"What do you know of my struggles?" Her eyes held fire, but not the kind that warmed me. It, could, perhaps burn me. I pushed the coffee away.

"I don't need to know, because you didn't struggle to start this company. You had your dad's money, and an idea that probably thousands of others had, except they had no funds. Luckily, you have some bright minds in the company to keep the train chugging along." My own anger surprised me and yet, I continued, "Nice story, by the way. A garage startup. Works every time."

"Are you here to insult me, Mr. Shetty?" Her frostiness was unexpectedly stinging. Her eyes shot ice daggers at me. Not that it mattered to me. I liked the fight.

"Didn't plan to. But since we are putting this out in the open, I think you would be pleased to know that TechNotes would love to take the burden off you and buy Note Nirvana. At a respectable price - one that would give you a nice profit. You can then go back to your privileged life, while I can run my company without having to fight unfairly."

She inclined her head slightly with a smugness I didn't like. "Scared of a little competition, Mr. Shetty? Fascinating, considering TechNotes is number one in the market." She snapped her fingers, her eyes lighting up suddenly. "Guess you got lucky with some smart minds too."

I stood abruptly, the metal chair making a loud scraping noise on the floor. The couple next to us looked alarmed. Nisha simply looked up, a small smile on her face.

I bent over, placing my hands on the table, and leaned closer. "I built the product myself. Every. Single. Feature."

She picked up her coffee as she stood up. I straightened, watching her come around the table and stood directly facing me. "So, did I, Mr. Shetty. So, did I." She moved around me to leave.

"My lawyers will be in touch to cut you a deal," I said, as I balled my hands into fists in my pocket.

She stopped abruptly and looked back, her eyes shining with challenge. I didn't know what made me say that.

"Lawyers are expensive. Save your cash for the upcoming bad days." I sucked in a breath as she smiled brightly. Her face betrayed no bitterness. "And oh, thanks again for the coffee."

I watched her weave out through the crowd, her heels making an irritating click on the wooden floor. *Oh, how I would enjoy destroying Note Nirvana.* I stormed out of the coffee shop, discarding my own coffee in the trash bin. Blinded by rage, I bumped into a couple on the street. I muttered my apologies, but all I could see in front of me was her mocking smile. I swore angrily under my breath. What did she even know about struggling? I survived on ramen noodles for a year straight, just to save enough cash to freaking buy pens for my employees. She probably had the most expensive pens in the world just lying around in her house!

I paced through the crowded sidewalks. The crisp September air did nothing to cool my temper. I was glad I wasn't being stifled by a tie right then. I stood with the huge crowd waiting to cross the street. The traffic light had just turned green for pedestrians when I heard someone call out my name. I pretended *not* to hear. I would have recognized that voice anywhere. This was *so* not the time for me to speak to Gus Reeves. Gus was the equivalent of a page three reporter in my world. He had been great for TechNotes in the past, publishing free glowing reviews of my company. Lately, however, I could sense his restlessness to get to some meatier news. Our PR team had been avoiding him like the plague, especially with everything that was happening with Nisha's product launch, but he was one persistent pest.

I sped up, hoping to lose him in the crowd, when I heard him again. I stopped abruptly. The two teenagers I bumped into moved around me, muttering "sorry" without even looking up from their smartphones. *Great.* Gus walked up to me with a big smile on his face. He had his casual t-shirt and jeans on, while his trusted iPad rested in the crossbody bag he had carried for the three years I had known him. He made an excellent first impression. His baby face lent him an innocence that people trusted. And yet, his gossip columns had resulted in companies closing down.

He greeted me with extended arms and a smile that would pass for affection - if you didn't know him well enough. The strangers around me probably thought we were long lost friends. I pried myself out of his tight hug and slapped him on the back.

"Arav Shetty, the sneaky billionaire! I am fed up with your disappearing acts."

I barked out a laugh. "Been a few busy days."

"Months. Few busy months. Do you know how long I have been chasing your PR people for an interview with you? nine fricking weeks. I thought we were friends." He pouted his fleshy lips and I wanted to throw up. His slyness made me nauseous. This was not a conversation I wanted to have after my terrible meeting with Nisha Jain.

"Sorry man. I will talk to our PR. Let's do it. Soon. I have to rush, though. It's been quite busy lately." I patted his back for good measure.

"You mean with Note Nirvana kicking your can? Is Nisha

Jain giving you nightmares?" He snickered, folding his arms. I resented his tone. I resented his insinuation that we were failing. I resented everything about him right then, and everything about Note Nirvana. I gritted my teeth, reining in the rage I felt inside.

"That's going to be fixed soon." I turned to leave, nodding him farewell.

"So that's what this meeting with Ms. Jain was all about? Are you cutting a deal? It didn't look like it went that well." I stopped in my tracks, my pulse racing.

I heard the snicker in his voice. Hands in fists, I was ready to punch him. How much did he know? And how did he know about the meeting? Would Nisha leak this out just to humiliate me? That was unlikely. It hadn't even been a full five minutes since I last saw that smug face of hers. I took a deep, cleansing breath before facing him.

"I am not commenting on speculation, Gus." I started walking away, when he rushed to join me, his short legs not quite keeping pace with my long strides.

"Off the record. Nothing is ever going to print," he said, panting slightly.

I shook my head. I plastered a convincing smile on my face and turned to him. I didn't want him to add me to his enemy list.

"How bad was it? Come on. Is she really as bad a pain in the neck as everyone says?" There was pleading in his voice; a desperate need to get hold of some gossip.

"What, you haven't interviewed her yet?" I asked, trying to route him to Nisha instead. Oddly, he didn't look insulted.

"Her PR has been stonewalling me since day one. I am considered an unspeakable evil in there," he said, rolling his eyes. It was an apt description of him, to be honest. "Anyway, is she taking you down?"

I tried to look casual, but anger was simmering just under my skin. "Dude, what have you been smoking? Tech-Notes is going pretty strong, and it will continue to do so. And-"

"And yet, you're desperate enough to meet Ms. Jain in private. I don't see *that* as going strong." He raised his eyebrows for dramatic effect, and it hit the intended mark.

Familiar tendrils of humiliation curled in my stomach. I took a step closer to him, my six feet large frame hovering over his far shorter height.

"TechNotes is an established company, and a newbie like Note Nirvana cannot shake us." I paused. "And as for cutting a deal with Note Nirvana, my competition has always begged me to take over. The day will soon come when Nisha Jain will hand over her company to me with a smile. If I ever want to buy Note Nirvana, that is."

A slow smile spread across his face.

"I am familiar with the ways of our conqueror." He gave an exaggerated bow. "I'd love to spend more time with you. Should I book next Friday for an official interview? Somewhere more hospitable than the 64th street sidewalk?" I stepped back.

"I will let the team know you'll email them," I said. He nodded and gave me a salute as I walked away.

I felt clean again, away from Gus's prying eyes. I always felt odd around him, as if I were naked and he could see right through me. The rush of anger I felt during out exchange was replaced by an uncomfortable sense of fatigue. Gus had just made clear what the media had already started hinting about - the first crack to form in TechNotes. The first hint of vulnerability for this giant company.

THE YELLOW TAXI skidded to a stop next to the pavement. Directing the driver to take me home, I let my head rest on the velvety fabric of the taxi seat. I felt muddled, a thousand thoughts assaulting me. But to my utter horror, it was guilt that gnawed at me the most. Guilt from acting like a jerk. No matter how privileged Nisha was, she didn't deserve the way I spoke to her. My hands curled protectively around my phone, stopping myself from doing something stupid, like calling her. I need to think things through first.

After two hours of a muscle-aching workout in my home gym, I felt in control and ready to confront the Nisha situation. I hit the shower, cold water running down my back. Muscles clenched, the water shot to the sore spots on my body. I enjoyed the pain - little reminders of the intense workout I just completed. I also felt lighter, my head cleared of the angry haze I had seen as I walked out of the coffee shop earlier in the day.

Regret darkened my mood again as I thought back on my behavior. Nisha definitely deserved an apology from me. Rival or not, I needed to be nicer. But, I was afraid.

From the time our eyes met, I felt every movement of her acutely. The tension in the air had put me on edge and cornered me into looking for an escape from falling for the beauty sitting in front of me. I hadn't felt that dumbstruck in a long while. I was known for my smart negotiations, for heaven's sake. And there I was, tongue-tied in front of my arch-rival. I had lashed out, attempting to get back control, and it was stupid. I looked up, pushing my wet hair back. The water hit my face, and it felt good.

I could hear my phone ring in the room. Hesitantly, I cut my shower short to answer the call. It was my uncle.

"Hello *beta,* are you back home?" he asked, his tone unnaturally excited.

"Yes. Been a long day," I said, as I flopped on to the bed.

"Well, if you would call the first meeting a *long day,* should I just call them to call this whole thing off?" His voice had gone quieter.

"What are you talking about?" I sat up, confused by his choice of words.

"Your date with Nisha, of course," he said matter-of-factly.

I would be lying if I said I was anything less than shocked. "Why would I go on a date with Nisha Jain?"

"Because... wait...you haven't seen the girl's profile I sent you?"

I shook my head. "No, but how is this connec-" My eyes widened at the realization.

My heart sped up as I recalled my uncle's earlier description of her. Yale. Heads a company. Only I didn't know she headed the company I fight against every day. I sucked in a breath as the enormity of what I had done hit me in full force.

"Nisha was the girl you wanted me to meet. The one you hoped I would marry."

4

———

ARAV

I quickened my pace, climbing two steps at a time. I removed my suit jacket and loosened my tie, while continuing to jog up to the fourteenth floor to Nisha's office. So far, Nisha had refused to take my texts or calls. I wouldn't have taken mine, either after the way I behaved at our only meeting! But getting this doe-eyed beauty out of my mind was next to impossible. I probably would have found another excuse to meet her even without my uncle's bombshell. And what news that was! To think, he had been trying to match me up with my biggest rival all this time. It was ridiculous. If I hadn't met her yesterday, I would have rejected the match right away. There was no way I would entertain the idea of a business rival for marriage, especially one whose company was trying to kill mine.

Yet, Nisha was different. The moment she walked into the coffee shop, my heart had skipped a beat. Her walk held the grace of a budding queen, while her face was that of an angel's. I could remember every detail, like how she tucked her glossy, jet-black hair behind her ear as she looked for me, and how she chewed her lip when she was thinking.

The moment our eyes met, I knew she would mean more to me than just a rival. There was a strange current between us that I couldn't put my finger on. I had needed an excuse to move away from her, to sort my feelings out . I offered to buy coffee, hoping the temporary distance would bring some much-needed normalcy to the meeting . After all, I went there to offer to buy her company, not to fall in love with her. And then I screwed up! I thought I was negotiating tough, but I only came across as an arrogant jerk.

I pushed through the staircase door on the fourteenth floor and welcomed the cool air blasting through the air conditioning vents. I stood there, hands on hips, panting. Sweat rolled down my cheek and I dabbed it with my sleeve. I was parched. I needed a shower and some fresh clothes before I met Nisha. *Oh, well!*

I strode ahead and tailgated an employee as he swiped his card to enter the glass doors. I paused to notice the huge, golden mandala wallpaper in front of me. The Notes Nirvana logo was on a glass fitting and highlighted with accent lights. Nisha had style, with a side dish of drama. I made a mental note to introduce some drama to TechNotes as well. I looked around for the front desk, and noticed a well-groomed man smiling at me on the left. He openly checked me out.

With a hand on the desk, he looked up dreamily at me and said, "Hi there, I'm Drew. You look lost. Are you here for an interview?"

Interview? Ha, more like I was here to beg for the job after screwing *up* the interview.

"No. Not yet, anyway. I own a company that was doing quite okay until...well, until you guys launched." I rested my arms on the front desk. "I am here to see Nisha."

He gave a lopsided smile and picked up the phone.

"Hey Steph, do you have an appointment for Nisha with Mr..." Drew raised a perfectly shaped eyebrow at me.

"Arav Shetty"

The phone almost slipped from his hand as he looked at me, shocked. I smiled wider, while his smile vanished completely. It took him about two minutes to confirm that I did not have an appointment. A look of utter resentment masked his perfect face now.

"You don't have an appointment, and Nisha is in a meeting right now. So, she can't meet you."

"No worries. I will wait here," I said, as I settled on the white visitor's couch for and rolled up my sleeves.

"Oh, she is going to be really, really late."

"I should be ok here," I said, patting the couch's soft cushions.

Drew stood up and walked around the front desk, agitated. Hands on hips and lips pursed, he seemed to struggle with what to say next.

"Did anyone ever tell you you are a bad liar?" I asked him.

He huffed and came closer. He was dressed like a complete professional, except for his rebellious red shoes.

"She doesn't *want* to see you. You should leave," he said through his teeth.

I admired his loyalty, but I didn't climb fourteen floors to walk back empty-handed to the elevator.

"She isn't in a meeting right now, is she?" I asked.

Drew straightened and crossed his arms defiantly. I stood up. I was only a few inches taller than him, but definitely better built. I looked behind him towards the narrow corridor, which had wall-to-wall posters of Note Nirvana's marketing ads. To the left of the front desk was the engineering team. I could hear the buzzing of conversation and the intense clacking of keys. I kept my engineering team as close to me as possible. After all, they were the brains behind the app. Maybe Nisha thought like me. Curiosity propelled my steps, and I took off toward the left.

"Hey...excuse me. You can't do that..." I heard Drew's voice behind me. "Stop...will you please?"

His voice trailed as everyone looked at me. I could see recognition in some faces, while others just stared at me shocked. "Goodness, can't even get him arrested. What a media story *that* would be...."

I could hear Drew coming closer again, and I quickened my pace. I quickly checked each conference room, looking around for Nisha's familiar face. I was wrong on so many levels for doing this. Here I was, her biggest business rival, in the heart of her business - if I paid enough attention, I would certainly stumble upon some secrets. I shut my eyes and shook my head. This was not about business. I was here to meet Nisha the woman, not the CEO.

I was almost at the end of the corridor, and it was a dead end. If this last conference room was not her office, I might end up escorted out by security. The hurried steps behind me were getting closer.

With no time to waste, I pushed open the heavy wooden door to the conference room, only to land right in the middle of a meeting of over twenty people. The room was dark, illuminated only by a bright projector screen. I stared at the woman presenting and immediately recognized her. Calista Wein, the brilliant, ever-slippery prized catch in the app product world was gaping at me, her mouth opening and closing like a fish. Then, she sprang into action. She scrambled to her laptop and shut it down immediately, the projector screen shutting off behind her. The room's lights came on and I squinted, adjusting my eyes to the brightness of the room.

"Arav?" Ah, there she was. Nisha was standing at the other end of the table, shock written all over her face. Her burgundy boatneck sheath dress hugged her curves in all the right places. Her long hair was in a messy bun, held up by a pen. "What are you doing here? Did you just walk...where is Drew?"

As if summoned by superior powers, Drew burst through the door panting, with a security guard behind him.

"Really?" I asked. I couldn't believe he was prepared to invite the media's crazy dance, just to stop me from seeing Nisha.

Drew just shrugged. "You asked for it." He walked to stand in front of me, facing Nisha. "I tried to stop him, but he just took off like his clothes were on fire."

He snickered, looking me up and down again as if he *wished* my clothes were on fire. Nisha gave me an incredulous look, her eyes wide, color rising in her cheeks.

"I can explain," I said, raising my hands in surrender. I didn't need any more drama. I just needed a few minutes with her. She huffed audibly. She walked briskly to the door, passing by me. When she reached the door, she turned around and said to the people in the room, "Five minutes. You guys can take a break."

Not missing the hint, I followed her and soon matched her pace. She took a quick right turn and entered a conference room. I followed her inside. It was smaller than the previous room, with a circular table in the middle that had four chairs around it. When the glass door closed shut, the room was bathed in pin-drop silence. I stood at one end, my suit jacket still in my hand, smiling like a fool.

"What's funny about this, Mr. Shetty?" Eyebrows propped, her look was a challenge. I wanted to rise to it, but I didn't want to waste the four minutes I had left squabbling with her.

"You didn't return my calls or texts. So, I had to come here. It's your fault really."

"Wow. After the way you insulted me, you really expected me to *want* to take your calls?" She asked, dislike evident on her face.

I shut my eyes, cringing at the memory of how badly I had behaved. I deserved her contempt.

"I know. I am sorry about that. I really am... and I cannot tell you how badly I felt after Krish uncle told me about us."

"Us?" she pointed at both of us.

Confusion marred her smooth forehead. I rubbed the tense muscles at the back of my neck as I realized I never really thought about how to break the news about my uncle's matchmaking prowess.

"Nisha, my uncle and your grandma..."

"My grandma?" Her eyes popped open wider.

I nodded. "My uncle and your grandma think we would be perfect for each other. My uncle emailed me your profile last week, but with the crisis at TechNotes - thanks to you" a smug smile cracked through her stiff profile, "I totally forgot to read that email. And then, yesterday, Krish uncle called Ryan and-"

"Wait, who's Ryan?" she asked.

"Oh sorry, Ryan is my best friend and TechNotes' CFO. He told my uncle that I was meeting you. So, my uncle called me in the evening to ask how my *date with you* went." I paused as I watched blush rise to her cheeks. I wanted an encore of *that*. "Well, that's when it struck me that you were the girl I was supposed to meet. But for an entirely different reason!"

She nodded, unable to meet my eyes. Her anger seemed to have been replaced by something else entirely. She held onto the chair, as if she needed the support.

"Matchmaking is my family's hobby, I must admit, " she said, nibbling at her lips.

My eyes moved to her lips. She stopped immediately and cleared her throat. "So? What now?"

The question caught me off guard. What now? I didn't know. I liked her and definitely wanted to see where this went. But, the way she threw the question at me made me nervous. I gripped the back of the chair in front of me. What was I thinking? That she would jump at a chance to explore a relationship, or agree to marry me after the way I insulted her yesterday? I sighed, defeated, the adrenaline finally leaving me.

"I guess we can give it a chance and see where it goes?" I finally said, hope refusing to leave my side. I just couldn't ignore the sparks we had when we met yesterday.

To my surprise, she was considering it, nibbling her lower lip once again. I struggled not to stare at those rosy lips and wonder what it would be like to kiss them.

"Why do you want to give it a chance? You think I am a spoiled brat living on my dad's riches. I didn't peg you for a gold-digger." she said, the bite back in her tone. She leaned back on the glass wall, her arms crossed again. "Maybe you think you are going to merge Note Nirvana after the marriage, and free me from the burdens of managing this company. And while I rest at some fancy house of ours, *you* take TechNotes to greater heights."

Her breathing was heavy, anger coloring her cheeks a different shade of pink. I didn't want an encore of *that.* I debated whether I should just walk out now, because she clearly had no interest in my proposition. I knew a lost deal when I see one, and this was beyond lost. This was a disaster.

Yet, I was unable to move. My heart was lodged in my throat, and I found myself speechless. The woman in front of me was one-of-a-kind. Smart, confident and beautiful. She made my heart sing with just a look, and right now, my heart was singing a whole opera. I wanted to fight for this woman. I needed to fight for her, for us, for a chance. It wasn't difficult for me to make a decision when I knew what I wanted.

"If that's what you fear, let me make it clear that I would never take the cowardly way of marrying you just to get your company. I would buy it for what it's worth."

She took a sharp breath and pushed herself off the wall. "I am not selling it to you."

"Fair enough. I am not buying it, until you show an interest in selling it."

"Not happening," she said, her tone sharp. I raised my hands in surrender.

"Got it." I paused. Her expression softened, and I grabbed the opportunity. "Now can we think about giving this a chance? We had a bad first meeting that was all business. We should meet again and just get to know each other, to see if we are a good match."

"But why?"

"Because I like you." I took a step closer, leaving just enough room for a single chair between us. "My rudeness to you yesterday, was partly because I couldn't believe I was thinking about how much I like you instead of focusing on business." Ah, there was that blush again, and for the umpteenth time, I wanted to feel the heat of her cheek under my fingers. "I think we may be good for each other." I paused, hope making me bolder. "You didn't feel it, too? The tension, the thickness of air between us yesterday? Or even now? Aren't you even a little curious to see if this means something?"

My heart hammered in my chest. I saw hesitation in her eyes, and I wondered if this attraction was all just my imagination. She looked down at her feet and pushed her hair behind her ears. I contemplated just walking out before my ego was crushed to powder under her black stilettos. I held my breath as she looked up and swallowed.

"OK," she said nodding.

"OK what?" My heart felt clogged up.

"We can give it a chance but-"

"Yes." She raised her eyebrows, mirth dancing in her dark eyes. "Whatever your conditions are, I agree to them."

"I have no conditions. Okay, maybe one." She paused, biting that perfect lip again. "Don't mix business with our relationship here. And, I want you to meet my grandma tonight, if you are available. She needs to see how wrong we are for each other."

She gave her first smile since I barged into her meeting and it felt like sunshine, beautiful and brilliant. I felt as though I could hold on to that image for the rest of my life and not feel even a pinch of pain ever again. I put my hands on my hips and nodded.

"Let's show your grandma her scheming ways are not going to work," I said, winking. I thought I saw a hint of that favorite color of mine on her face again, but she quickly looked away and checked her watch.

"I am three minutes late, Arav. One thing you should know about me is that I hate being late."

"That makes two of us. Punctuality. Check." I opened the

door for her and she walked out, a smile tugging at her perfect lips.

"I leave work at six. I will text you my address and we can meet at the front gate?" Thanks to Ryan's minions, I already knew her address, but, of course, I didn't tell her that. Instead, I simply nodded. We walked back to her conference room together and found Drew waiting, iPad in hand, lounging lazily against the wall.

"Worried I would kidnap your boss?" I said, teasing.

He held up a mocking eyebrow. "More like I'm worried about having to clean up the blood after she murdered you."

"Drew!" Nisha chided him, but he continued giving me a murderous look. I liked him. This kind of loyalty was good for her.

"See you later then?" I said. She nodded, her soft eyes, stirring something in me. I turned around, wondering how much more I could take in a single day.

BY THE TIME I reached Nisha's place, I had showered, changed and put on a good amount of deodorant, in case I had to climb any more stairs to get to her. I sat in my BMW waiting, caressing the leather steering wheel. Nisha would be there any minute, according to her text.

I stared at the stone fence. The ivy vines all over it reminded me of castles and forts. Her *house* was no less than a castle – a huge stone mansion that rose up behind the fence, with a half-mile long driveway in front of it. Kamlesh Jain sure knew how to make a statement about his wealth. I wondered if he was also part of the discussions my uncle had with Nisha's grandma.

I had never met Kamlesh Jain but I had heard enough

about the real estate tycoon to know that he valued family money over rags-to-riches acquisition. I was no rags-to-riches story, but I also didn't come from a family with pots of gold. We were always well-off enough to afford some luxuries, thanks to my dad's business in India, but we were never rich enough to have our own *castle*.

Just as I began to doubt whether this match would be a good idea after all, bright lights from behind me blinded me for a moment. Nisha's black Audi crept up beside my car, and she nodded at me and pointed to the massive closed iron gates. The gates creaked open as her car slowly pulled inside onto the driveway, and I followed suit.

Even at seven-thirty in the evening, it was bright enough for me to notice the well-manicured lawns on both sides of the driveway, which were smattered with bushes of colorful flowers. As we moved in, the true enormity of the stone mansion dawned on me. It reminded me of one of the palaces I once visited in Rhode Island when I was eighteen. I recalled walking through the huge rooms and thinking I would never live in such a huge place, even if I had all the money in the world.

My Manhattan penthouse apartment might just fit into this mansion's parking lot. Nisha and I really did come from different worlds. I wondered about how our differences would allow us to make a life together. I took a deep, calming breath and pushed my doubts aside. *Too soon*, I told myself.

Nisha was already waiting by her car when I strolled to her. "Hope you are ready. My grandma is not subtle about anything in life." A smile lit her eyes.

"I already like her," I said, following her inside.

Her laughter echoed in the hallway as we entered the mansion through the hug teak double doors, which were already open. We walked through a massive hallway flanked by a curved stairway on both sides. The hallway had two living spaces with leather couches. There was no one occupying them, and the tapping of our shoes created a ghostly echo within the walls.

"This is where we have guests. You can usually find Dad, at the bar, over there." She pointed to a huge bar that occupied the whole wall. There was no bartender right then, but I could not image Mr. Jain tending his own bar. "Let's go upstairs. She's probably in her room or on the terrace." I nodded once and followed her.

The upstairs was equally huge, but had doors to individual rooms. It was exactly like one of those Rhode Island palaces, and I cringed internally. How did one live in such huge spaces? Nisha stopped at a door at the far end and knocked. There was no answer, so she kept walking to the door next to it. When she opened it, to my surprise, there was no room; instead a long veranda with floor-to-ceiling windows opened up to a massive terrace. Out there on one of several lounge chairs was a woman with a book.

Nisha walked to her left and opened the door to the terrace. Hair as white as it could be, her grandma looked rested and lost in her reading. I was close enough to see the half-naked man in military pants on the book cover, and I looked at Nisha just in time to see her rolling her eyes at it.

"So, on a scale of ten, how steamy is this book?" Nisha said bending her head slightly to get a closer look. "Hmm, OK. It had better live up to *that* title!"

Her grandma's musical laughter came first. Then she laid her eyes on Nisha, and happiness showed in her creased skin. Age didn't seem to mar the beauty she must have been in her youth.

"Twelve so far, but the hero has started to sound wimpy. So, we will see," her grandma declared.

She stood and stretched out her arms to Nisha. Nisha hugged her, fondness pouring out of her. Though shorter than Nisha's five-feet seven inches, her grandma rose up on her toes and kissed her forehead. She reminded me of my aunt Seema. She never passed up a chance to hug us.

"I see you brought Arav with you," she said, looking at me. She beckoned me to come closer with a wave. As I took a step closer to her, she looked me up and down. She squeezed my shoulders and said, "Such a handsome boy. Fire your photographer. He doesn't do you any justice. You look so much better in real life."

Laughter burst out of me. I sure was basking in her grandmotherly attention.

"I am Sohni, by the way," she said, though it wasn't necessary.

She turned to Nisha and said, "If you are here for my blessing, then it's done. Tell me when would be a good time for the wedding, and I will get started."

Eyes wide, Nisha looked at both of us, shocked. "Grandma, I brought him here to show you what a mistake you have made. You know I am competing against his company. Why in the world would you think he is good for me?"

"Why in the world not? Don't you see how good looking he is? I would marry him if I was young enough." She winked at me.

"I would marry you even now. You are too sexy to pass up."

Her grandma rewarded me with her musical laughter again, and hit my shoulder playfully. Nisha rolled her eyes, though a smile tugged at her lips. This felt like home. I cleared my throat to steer the conversation toward the level of seriousness that I knew Nisha was looking for.

"We had a bad first meeting, Ma'am, and Nisha is not pleased to know you are trying to set her up with me." I said to Sohni.

"And are you pleased with my efforts?" She asked in a conspiring voice, but I knew she wanted sincerity from me.

"Extremely." Softness returned to Sohni's eyes, but only to be replaced by questions. "But I am afraid I made a very bad first impression," I finished.

"You are a good man. Charm your way into her heart, son. All that Nisha ever asks for is respect and sincere love."

We both heard Nisha noisily clearing her throat, attracting our attention to her. I filed away Sonhi's advice in my memory.

"If you are done exchanging notes, I am right here, objecting to this match. Grandma, we are business rivals. Did you consider the possibility of cold-blooded murder before we even get to the wedding hall??" Nisha plopped down on the lounge chair just vacated by her grandma and sighed. I stood with my hands in my pockets and watched as Sohni took slow steps towards her granddaughter. She put a hand on Nisha's head, stroking her beautiful hair.

"You would be surprised how much more exciting life is when you have a partner who is nothing like you and yet is everything you need." She paused. "You are both independent and you both built your own companies successfully from the ground up. I felt you both were driven by the same fire. No harm in finding out if that's true, right?"

Nisha looked at her grandmother, worry creasing her forehead. I wondered what was it that bothered her so much about me. I got the business competition part, but it felt like more than that.

"I am not ready yet. Nik is still-"

"I would talk to Kamlesh about him." Sohni continued stroking Nisha's hair.

Nisha looked at me, her gaze soft but full of doubt. I looked straight at her, willing her to give us a fair chance - not a half-hearted one. She pursed her lips, the uncertainty in her eyes seeming to win over any inclination she had toward me.

Suddenly, she was no longer looking at me, her attention drawn instead to someone behind me. Her eyes turned hard and she stood suddenly, arms stiff at her side. I turned to see who it was and froze. Kamlesh Jain was standing at the entrance, a glass of amber liquid in one hand and the other hand tucked in his suit pant pocket. Kamlesh Jain, - whose brand garners enough moolah to pay for a month's salary for all my employees - wasn't smiling either.

"Ah Kamlesh, good timing. Look who Nisha brought home," Sohni declared, breaking the cold silence in the air. I breathed out a sigh of relief, even though I was going to be the subject of Kamlesh Jain's scrutiny.

"And who do we have here?" The authority in his voice matched his reputation. It was my turn to make an impression.

"Arav Shetty, sir." I shook his hand and stepped back. There was no smile in return, only scrutiny and mistrust written on his face.

"And?" He inclined his head slightly. My name was not enough for an introduction.

"CEO, TechNotes."

"A dotcom company. What's your annual revenue?" I was about to respond to the unusual, hostile interrogation when I was interrupted by Nisha.

"Don't bother answering that, Arav. My Dad thinks no

dotcom company is worth his attention. They are all bubbles that burst sooner rather than later." Nisha stood by my side and I began to understand some of the animosity that seemed to exist between father and daughter.

"Well, they did burst in 2000, and will again. Old money is proven." His tone was casual, but his eyes on Nisha were stern.

Nisha, on the other hand, just grew more agitated. She was spoiling for a fight and was about to reply when Sohni interrupted.

"I talked to Arav's uncle Krish recently and felt he is a good match for Nisha." Kamlesh looked back at me, eyes holding renewed interest.

Nisha wore her defiance on her sleeve, and he didn't look pleased.

"What are your plans for breakfast tomorrow, son?" The question took me aback.

I had a meeting with Ryan and the finance team about the year's budget, but I knew this would be my only chance at making an impression on Nisha's father.

"I have a meeting, but I can move it to later in the day."

He nodded and said, "Good. See you at seven thirty in the morning tomorrow." Saying thus, he turned toward the door to leave. He had taken two steps when he stopped and looked back. "And, oh, Nisha, Nikhil called, and I gave him permission to pick you up as his date for Sean's wedding. Just so you know."

His eyes held a warning, and for the second time, I felt rage at this Nikhil person. Was he her ex-boyfriend? Nisha stiffened beside me. Just as he turned back, I heard her breathe out in a rush.

"No," she said. Her father turned back, eyebrows turned up in question. "I already have a date."

Nisha scooted closer to me and looped her arm in mine. I masked my shock and looked at her father, my poker face on. "I am going with Arav." She looked at me, smiling, eyes pleading with me to play along. I smiled back at her warmly.

"It would be my honor, sir, to accompany your daughter to the wedding." I stood straighter, looking in the eye of Kamlesh Jain. I didn't have to fake sincerity. I meant every word. His eyes looked hesitant as they moved from our looped arms to his daughter's defiant face. He paused and looked behind us at his mother, as if to confirm his decision. From the corner of my eye, I saw Sohni giving a slight nod and I held my breath.

"I will inform Nikhil." He nodded once at me and left the terrace as suddenly as he arrived. Nisha visibly slumped and the tense air around us loosened. Kamlesh Jain had raw power, and I found I already had no appetite for tomorrow's breakfast.

"Thank you." Nisha whispered, looking away. She hugged her grandma, who in turn, patted her back.

"Arav, you better bring your ace game to the breakfast tomorrow. Kamlesh will skin you alive if he finds you taking advantage of my dear granddaughter".

"My intentions are all honorable, ma'am. All honorable." I said as both the beautiful women in front of me broke into laughter.

Nisha's eyes met mine, and I found warmth in in hers. I had passed some sort of test in her mind, and I was glad I had. If I wanted to charm her, I would have to charm her father first. And, if there was any possibility of getting Nisha to look at me like I was her shining knight in armor again, I was ready to face Kamlesh Jain head on.

5

———

ARAV

I gazed at the acres of green spread in front of me. The sun's soft morning rays cast a golden glow on whatever part of the field was not darkened by the mansion's shadow. I shifted to look around at the room, observing the golden wallpaper, the crystal chandeliers, and the long creamy curtains accenting the floor-to-ceiling windows, which blocked out the crisp morning air. I wanted to walk out of this stuffy breakfast room, and walk across the lawn to the little pond that I could see at the far end. It had been a long time since I had enjoyed nature properly. The concrete jungle of Manhattan didn't offer many such chances. Instead, I was waiting here for Kamlesh Jain and the interrogation that Sohni promised.

A part of me also wondered what brought me here. Only a couple of days before, I was at the coffee shop meeting my archrival for the very first time. I was smitten, but fighting it hard, insulting and infuriating her to the extent that she refused to acknowledge my existence. And yet I was here today, about to talk to her father about my suitability to marry his daughter if she so chose. *If she so chose.* What if she didn't? I gritted my teeth, quelling the possibility. I had almost never lost a battle, and winning Nisha's heart was way more than some conquest. She was not a battle to be won. She was the companion I wanted by my side in my battles.

It wasn't that I was in love with her. Not yet, anyway. But every fiber of my being screamed she was the right one for me. Even when I met her at the coffee shop, when I had no idea my uncle had these grand plans for us, my thoughts had turned treacherous, wondering about what lay beneath the surface of this doe-eyed beauty. I wanted to know more about her. I *needed* to know her. The pull was different and stronger than I had ever felt for anyone else. And yet, I could not claim I was in love with her. Not yet, but I definitely wanted to try. Loving Nisha Jain would be one hell of a ride.

I turned around at the sound of footsteps. Kamlesh Jain marched into the room, his tailored dark blue suit lending a sharpness to his profile. He must have been at least sixty years old, but his energy would rival that of an eighteen-year old. I stood, waiting, while he settled on the rich, cream-colored leather dining chair, which was accentuated by brass nail head trim. He did not acknowledge my presence. He picked up a piece of crisp toast from his plate and smeared enough Nutella on it to last me a full month. I watched as he bit off a piece; the crunch of the toast was audible even at that distance.

"I read some interesting background on your father yesterday." I tensed. His choice of words cut off air from my lungs. He looked at me, his expression unreadable. "A businessman with moderate success until the age of forty-five, when he suddenly retires. That's when you moved to The

United States. Alone. Leaving your parents back in India." I refused to look away as he watched me. I steeled myself against what was coming. "Businessman. Drunkard. Wife beater." I flinched, and lost the battle. No matter how prepared you are, it's still a punch in the gut when the horrible truth is thrown at your face. I breathed heavily; the weight of my father's sin was too heavy a burden to carry. Shame overpowered my senses. I couldn't bear to stand there for even a moment. I strode around the dining table towards the door, and then I heard his soft laughter. "Like father, like son, are we?"

"I am *nothing* like my father!" I spun around, panting, my voice reverberating in the tall ceiling of the dining room. "My mother sent me away from him to be a better man, and every second of every day since I left my home, I have stood by my promise. I am NOT my father." He sat calmly, with his elbows propped up on the table and his hands under his chin, his face giving away nothing. At that moment, I didn't care if he didn't want to give his daughter's hand in marriage, but I did care that he was trying to equate me to my father. That, I couldn't live with.

"I see the same success, same anger in you." My fingers curled into a fist and my breathing hitched. The rational part of me whispered that he was goading me into a scene. And yet, anger pulsed in my veins. In that instant, I could have punched him in the face, but then I would, indeed, be my father's son.

I breathed slowly, and just like I had in the past, I reminded myself why I would never succumb to anger. I engulfed myself with the sweet memories of my mother, her smile and sacrifice giving my anger a way out. She didn't die in vain. She didn't give me up, only to have me turn into someone just like her husband. I made her proud. The last time I spoke to her before her death, she was animated with happiness and pride. The thought of her finally made me feel calm, and my breath evened out. My mother's love was a thick cloak over that dark part of me.

"No sir. My company's success was all me. building it from the ground up and making my unique mark on the world." For the first time, his eyes held emotion. For just a fleeting second, I saw solidarity and understanding. "As for the anger," I continued, "No man would stand quiet if the worst of his father's doing was being used as a yardstick for his own character. I wanted to yell out how different I am from him but then, my mother's carefully instilled manners told me I need to behave better."

He leaned back against the plush back of the dining chair and inclined his head, a silent encouragement to continue. I looked away from him, towards the rolling greens beyond the windows of the mansion. The manicured opulence of this place was nothing like the lush greenery and simple warmth I grew up with. The cool interiors of our house in India warmed my senses. I could almost touch the painted white brick walls that led to the kitchen, and to my mom, as she spent most of her time there. I could almost smell the aroma of the food she prepared. I had many memories of her, but the best were of her in the kitchen, and how happy it made her to cook for me, and chat with me while I sat in the breakfast nook, basking in her attention.

"Karan Shetty was a good man and a good father until his best friend and business partner cheated him out of his hard-earned money. He took to drinking and was never the same," I said, my voice gentler than I expected. Sadness crushed me from within, but I wasn't going to give Kamlesh anything to use against me. I stood up taller and fixed my eyes on his face. I wasn't afraid of being judged. "Having seen the ruin that a frail heart can bring into the lives of people I love, I am anything but weak. You can trust me on that."

Kamlesh uttered no words of disapproval, and none of solace. He was quiet, perhaps reconsidering his plans to pursue a match with his daughter. I wouldn't have been shocked if he didn't want this alliance anymore, especially if he knew how brutal my father was. We kept staring at each other, neither of us giving the other space to back off. I was doing everything on the "How NOT to impress your father-in-law" list. So, his next words almost gave me whiplash.

"Take a seat." He took another bite of his toast. A servant rushed in and placed a plate of food in front of me, adding still more to the variety of options already presented on the table. I kept myself from rolling my eyes at the show Kamlesh was putting on for me. I wasn't a stranger to luxuries, but I guessed that this was his style of intimidation. I served myself a bowl of cereal and some cold milk. He followed my every movement while I studiously ignored him. After what felt like an eternity, he cleared his throat. I looked up, and he gave me a small smile. "Of all that's offered, that's what you choose to eat?" He said pointing at my cereal bowl.

"I am easy to please," I said, giving him a small smile of my own. He shook his head and started laughing in earnest. I stopped eating to watch the miracle of making Kamlesh Jain laugh loud and long enough to see tears flowing down the sides of his tanned, plump cheeks. When he finally quieted down, he looked pleased right to the bone.

"I am beginning to wonder if you are truly the right match for Nisha. You are both more similar than I would like to admit, frankly," he said, still smiling. I marveled at how handsome his aged face looked. The resemblance between him and Nisha seemed stronger now.

"How so, sir?" He looked at me without really looking at me, a glimmer of fondness in his eyes. Distant, fond memories seemed to have taken over.

"Nisha would reject all the big, expensive toys I got for her, while playing endlessly with the cardboard boxes they came in always. It took me a while to understand why. As a father, it was hard not to be hurt. I felt inadequate. One day, I just brought her an empty box. The boisterous laugh that she gave me that day is a sound I will never forget. I ended up spending the whole evening with her. I even forgot about a couple of meetings I had. Later that night, as I marveled to my wife that our daughter wanted nothing but a box, she burst out laughing. She said, *'It's not the box, Kamlesh. It's you.'*"

He looked at me, eyes still glazed, a sad smile playing on his lips. "Now, she refuses to even acknowledge me because I offered her another expensive gift instead of my faith in her." He must have observed the confusion on my face. "Nisha refused to take even a single penny that I gave her for her company," he explained. "She built Note Nirvana with her own money, that she earned while working as a research assistant at Yale University. Just like you, she built it from nothing, and made it something beautiful."

I felt the ground slip under my feet. Nisha's company was not funded by her dad? That explained why she was so infuriated when I suggested as much in our first meeting. I hit her where it hurts the most.

"I wasn't aware of that." I wanted to kick myself hard. How was I going to make it up to her now? He nodded. Dabbing his lips, he stood to leave, and I stood up too.

"I give you my blessing to pursue the alliance and see if

you both feel this is a good match. I will talk to your uncle about it." He took a step closer and shook my hand. I nodded my thanks. He was still gripping my hand when he added, "If you ever hurt my daughter, I promise you a very painful death."

6

NISHA

My father strode across the hallway while I sat at the breakfast bar stool with my orange juice. I noticed the absence of rage, which automatically meant he was pleased. Arav followed him a few paces behind, in unhurried steps down the staircase. From where I was sitting, hidden by the beam separating the hallway and breakfast bar, I could watch Arav undetected. He was in his trademark perfectly fitting suit - a grey one today, with a white tie. He didn't look pleased, and I wondered if my dad was doing what he does best - making people extremely uncomfortable. He paused midway on the staircase, seemingly lost in thought. Then he took out his phone and started typing.

My thoughts went to the last text he sent after he left my place last night. A single question - *Who is Nikhil?* Of all things that happened yesterday, only one thing bothered him - competition. So typically male. I rolled my eyes, sipped my juice and continued watching him. I had to admit he was quite pleasing to the eye. He continued typing with one hand while the other rested on his hip. There was a sense of unrest in him today, and it was fascinating to watch him struggle with it. But then, he stopped typing. He looked up at the ceiling, frustration pinching his features. He cursed softly, and my interest was piqued. I tried to remember if there were any major morning press releases from Note Nirvana that could hit TechNotes numbers today, but none came to mind. We would have a bombshell of product release in a couple of months, which was guaranteed to rile him up, but this was not the time to worry about that.

His attention turned back to his phone. His hands decisively typed something, and he put the phone to his ear. He was calling someone. I jumped as my phone blared Ed Sheeran's "Shape of You" song, then cringed as the music echoed in the empty hallway. He would surely know now that I was watching him. I heard his heavy footsteps down the staircase as I silenced my phone. He appeared from behind the pillar looking nothing but pleased. There was no trace of the frustration that I witnessed earlier.

"Nice ringtone." He took a seat next to me, his body angled towards me. I tried not to notice how the shirt contoured his hard pecs.

"My niece put it on my phone last week. I forgot to change it." He looked surprised.

"I didn't know you had siblings." There was something in his eyes that was different today. They shone with an empathy I couldn't understand.

"Two older sisters. The eldest, Sara, is married with two kids. Anshi, my middle sister," I swallowed the lump that rose at just a mention of her name, "is in rehab, recovering from a drug addiction." I stared at my half-finished glass of juice, my appetite gone. It had been three months since I had seen Anshi, and every day I felt like I was losing her more to insanity. Arav angled his stool further towards me, and the sweet tension between us drove all thoughts of Anshi out the door.

"You didn't have to tell me that," he said. I shrugged, my thoughts muddled with his proximity. There was a long pause. Long enough to wonder if he felt the same buzz that I felt. His thighs were just a hair-length away. The sweet heat I felt kept me rooted to my seat. "Why didn't you tell me you were self-funded when I accused you of being a spoiled brat?" he asked. His voice was soft and laced with guilt. When I looked up, I found him staring at me. His brown eyes met mine, and I was unable to look away. Why didn't I tell him the truth? Why didn't I stop him as he accused me of having an easy life when he knew nothing of my struggles?

"Because it was easier to hate you that way." Truth tumbled out in a whisper and I gasped. I hadn't intended to say that aloud.

His eyes widened just a little bit, but were immediately drawn to my lips. I gazed at his face - his sharp nose, his full lips slightly upturned at the end. His high cheekbones gave him an aristocratic look. I ached to be touched by him, to know how it would feel to be kissed by this stubborn man. I wet my parched lips. I let out a shudder as he caressed my cheek with the back of his hand. Then, ever so delicately, his thumb traced my cheekbone, while his hand cupped the right side of my face. His eyes held heat. I watched his Adam's apple bob as he swallowed and my lips parted. He was closer, his fingers sliding to the base of my neck while his thumb continued to caress my jaw and ear. He smelled of cinnamon, and my heart raced. I was unable to wait to get a taste of it. Even the sound of footfalls didn't curb the yearning for his touch. I moved my head slightly higher to reach his lips when he suddenly pushed me away. I gasped as I was knocked slightly off-balance on the bar stool, but he grabbed my hand tight and kept me from falling. He was already looking at the staircase as my grandma's voice carried through the hallway. She was doling out book recommendations to someone on the phone. When she saw us, she waved with a smile, but continued on her way. I sighed in relief. I was not in any shape to face an interrogation. What was I thinking?! Perhaps Arav felt the want as I did.

He rubbed his face. The soft whisper of skin against skin burned the embers of want brighter within me. A few locks of his cropped hair fell on his smooth forehead as he looked up at me, smiling. I curled my hands into fists, determined not to touch him.

"You are going to get me in trouble, my sweet doe." Heat pooled in my cheeks and I looked away. I felt him closer, heat from his body like a siren's song. "Nisha, look at me please." I hesitated. I hadn't agreed to this marriage alliance - complexities abounded with this match - and yet, everything just felt so right with him. "I want to take you on a proper date. We can get to know each other better. You know nothing about me, while I have been taking quite a few notes about you from your grandma and your dad." At that, I turned and was rewarded by a cocky, lopsided smile. For once, I don't want to swipe it off his face. "And then, we can decide if we want to get married."

"Sounds fair. Does this mean my dad is okay with this?" I asked, wagging my finger in the space between us. He nodded, and his smile dimmed somewhat. I wondered what happened between them.

"How does Friday sound? I don't want to go to that

wedding date on Saturday without getting a full report on this Nikhil guy. You never replied to my text."

I rolled my eyes. "Friday is good. Pick me up after work at six. And, can you please put your caveman tendencies aside when you are with me?" He handed me my Louis Vuitton handbag as I alighted from the breakfast bar stool and adjusted my burgundy dress.

"Anything for you, sweet doe." I shook my head at his blatant flirtation while secretly repeating the pet name he had given me over and over again in my head.

7

ARAV

Ryan wasn't happy. He sat opposite to me, legs crossed ankle to knee, and pretended to listen to the financial analyst doling out numbers. Every few minutes he looked at me, eyes narrowed with accusation, and then looked away. But the worst part was that every time I asked a question, he rolled his eyes as if *I* was pretending to listen. Enough was enough.

"Can we do this tomorrow?" I said, abruptly. The financial analyst was taken aback, having been interrupted in the middle of a sentence. "I am sorry. Something urgent has come up." I looked at Ryan, who gave me the biggest eye roll yet. " Ryan, can you please stay back for a second?"

"Nah, I have to jump to an investor meeting-" His swagger was too much to take.

"Cancel the meeting. This is urgent." He tsked and played with his phone. There was no investor meeting. It was all a front to continue to show his displeasure with me.

"You can stop acting now. He's gone." I pointed to the empty room and the closed door. Eyebrows raised, Ryan faked confusion, and I wanted to punch him in the face.

"What's the deal with you today? Why are you acting like such a diva?" He uncrossed his legs and stood up, his chiseled face that women so love suddenly in my face.

"You're going into an arranged fricking *marriage with Nisha Jain*, and you didn't *bother* to tell me - as a best friend, *or* the CFO of this company?" Trust Ryan to get riled up like a girl over gossip. I held my position, staying eye to eye with him.

"I am having serious doubts about your competence as CFO right this minute. If gossip can make you question your boss, I wonder what damage our competitors can do with it." With a raised eyebrow, he took a step back. He nodded and scrolled through his phone. His smug smile returned, and he turned the screen toward me. It was a copy of my calendar, which I had shared with him. The morning was blocked with the title "*Meet Nisha's Dad*". I tried putting on my poker face, but he already had his answer. He threw the phone on the couch and crossed his arms, waiting for an explanation.

I raised my hands in surrender. "Okay. Let me start from the beginning".

"That sounds like a plan." He took a seat on my leather couch while I walked back to my desk. I slumped in to my chair, the strain of the morning's discussion with Nisha's father finally catching up with me.

"Remember that girl my uncle was trying to get me to talk with? Well it turned out to be Nisha. My uncle and Nisha's grandmother decided we would be perfect for each other, and they hatched this ridiculous plan." I pulled my legs up on to the mahogany desk and sighed. "I went to meet her dad to ensure he is okay with us getting to know each other."

"Us?" Ryan sat forward, his arms on his knees.

"Nisha and I, of course."

"She's okay with this?" He then pointed a finger at me. "Are *you* okay with this?" I ran my hands through my hair. If only I knew what I was doing. Marrying Nisha would come with complexities I couldn't even begin to comprehend, and yet, every time I thought of her, I ached to know more. I wanted to know what made those delicious lips smile, those doe eyes brighten, or that smooth-as-silk skin blush. I wanted to unravel the mystery that she seemed to hold in her chest. I needed to see her again, and Friday couldn't come soon enough. "I thought so." Ryan slumped back into his couch and I looked at him in confusion. "You are smitten, Romeo. TechNotes is going down. You're right. You do need to hire a new CFO because this guy," he said, pointing to himself, "is out the door."

"I am not marrying her. Yet." I added with a sigh. "I just got her dad's permission. We are going to see if we like each other first." I didn't feel the need to mention that I hoped like hell that we did.

"And what happens if you do like each other?" That was not a question I wanted to answer for now. I shrugged and rested my arms under my head. He rolled his eyes again, while his posture matched mine. "You'll have to merge TechNotes with Note Nirvana." I pondered that possibility. If Nisha was anything like me, she would hate the idea.

"She would break off this alliance." My statement was met with silence, and I knew that meant Ryan had his CFO hat on – which meant he was now all-business.

"Then we fall back on the original plan - buy Note Nirvana. And this time, you get to sleep with the beautiful owner too." He dodged as I threw the nearest pen at him. His boisterous laugh was too grating.

I shook my head, clearing out the sickening lovey-dovey

emotions that I was falling prey to. I needed to give this issue some serious thought. But for the first time, I was afraid to face the problem. I was afraid of the consequences if I took a wrong step. The fear of losing Nisha even before I got her was a nightmare. But maybe, just maybe if I offered the right price for her company, she would take it less violently than I anticipated?

My thoughts were interrupted by the shrill ring of Ryan's cell phone. With a sly smile, he left me alone. That must definitely have been his latest conquest calling. Good for him – he didn't have to deal with this arranged marriage crap. If he had to get married, his creativity in chasing the female species would definitely meet a stifling death.

Not long after he left, I received an excited text from my aunt, congratulating me for taking the first serious step towards knowing Nisha. She even mentioned that the rooftop of the luxury hotel *Peninsula* would be an excellent wedding venue. Oddly enough, the minute I read the words, I could just picture Nisha in golden bridal attire.

8

———

NISHA

As a young bride, my grandma was an equal partner in my granddad's real estate company. In those days, it was unheard of for a young Indian wife to play such an important role in business. But my grandma was known for her impressive social skills, which would often help my granddad negotiate his way up the chain with sophistication. Within ten short years, our family raised itself to be included in the top echelons of New York's successful real estate families.

While grandma started taking a backseat in business after granddad's death, she didn't take a backseat in life. She continued to be as kind and comforting as she always had been. She took a special interest in me, the strangely silent granddaughter in a house full of raucous kids and adults. She would often say I remind her of herself as a child. The only daughter out of eight children, she grew up compliant and quiet. Ironically, it was her arranged marriage with my granddad that set her free. Sadly though, she believed that's what I needed, too - a man who could set me free from my demons.

But a man was exactly what I didn't need. I preferred my solitary journey. I preferred fighting my battles alone, because every time I trusted a man to stand with me, he either pushed me behind, deeming me too weak to fight, or just left me alone. Nikhil was the latest example, treating my start-up company as a *hobby* that I indulged myself in to pass the time. I bristled at the thought.

Standing at the foot of my office building, I re-read the text grandma sent me in the morning about meeting Arav on our first date.

Remember to keep an open mind. Let the magic seep in.

Clearly, she'd been reading too many romance novels. The happily-ever-afters that entertained her during the day – and her own happily-ever-after - were something she wanted for me, too . But not everyone was as lucky as she was. Not everyone gets a kind, supportive husband like hers.

Loud drops of rain pattered the glass ceiling I was standing under. The sound was strangely calming. I preferred it over the chaos that my mind was in at this moment. It had been three days since Arav asked me out on a date. All I had been able to focus on since was his LinkedIn profile picture. Apart from that, I had waltzed through my days at work in a daze, imagining and re-imagining how tonight's date would go.

Arav was different than any other man I had met. Our almost-kiss had unraveled something within me. I was looking forward to spending time with him. There was something about the way he looked at me that let all of the butterflies in my belly loose and wild. How easy it was to give in to my desires with just a touch of his hand! My finger traced the lines of my cheek, reliving his hot touch. My breath hitched as I recalled every little speck of desire in his warm brown eyes. There were a thousand promises in those eyes -promises I dreamed of and wanted to believe in.

I was thankful for the light splatter of raindrops cooling my body. I exhaled a long breath and checked my watch. It was three in the afternoon, and Arav and I had decided to meet at the restaurant at six-thirty. Three more hours before I got to see him. Just a few more hours before the journey of disappointment began. Just like every other date I had been on before. I turned to walk back to my office, when I saw our VP of Network Security sprinting towards me. Alarm bells rang in my head, and all thoughts of Arav dissipated into nothing.

ED SHEERAN'S song blared loudly from my office while I sat on the floor of our Network and Security team office. I heard heavy footsteps behind me and turned to find Drew handing me my still-ringing phone. It was Arav. Startled, I quickly checked the time on my wristwatch and cursed. It was already seven thirty. The ringing stopped. He had called four times already, but it seemed we were all too occupied with the crisis to even hear the phone. I got up from the floor, making my way to my office quickly. I regretted having to tell him about today. He picked up on the first ring.

"Hey Nisha, are you okay?" A slight shiver ran through me as his deep voice registered. I found myself nodding before words formed on my lips.

"Yes," I cleared my hoarse throat, "I left my phone in the office. Sorry, I'm trying to put out some major fires at work here." There was silence on the other end, punctuated by the soft clicks of the car indicators. "Arav, you still there? Are you driving?"

"Ah yes. I was actually on my way to your office because...well...you weren't picking up my calls." I bit my lip. He was driving all the way from the other end of the city to check on me.

"Oh, you didn't have to, Arav. I am fine. I just can't make it to dinner today. I may have to pull an all-nighter here, actually. I am sorry I didn't call you sooner. We just lost track of time." Peter, our Network Security Admin, knocked softly and peeked in. I nodded at him. Things were not looking good at all and we needed all hands on deck. "I have to go, Arav. But we are still on for the wedding tomorrow, okay? See you at nine in the morning at my place?"

"OK. I will be there" I clutched my phone tighter, intensely regretting that I wouldn't be able to see him tonight.

"See you tomorrow, then. I will go-"

"Hey Nisha, wait."

"Yes"

"Can I...I mean I can...later maybe..."

"Later what?"

"Actually, never mind. You go fix that monster issue. I will see you tomorrow, ok...bye.". The soft click sounded much louder somehow, and I stared at my phone for a few seconds. Never had I heard Arav sound as uncertain as he did today. Thorny tendrils of want snaked through my heart again. I wanted to see him right then, to whisper the doubt in his mind away, to reassure him. But reassure him of what? Sounds from outside of my office distracted me, and I was grateful. I needed to focus on me, and my company. I had given enough to others.

~

"I'M CALLING SECURITY" Drew's panicked voice wafted through the long corridor. I looked up, blinking away tiredness from staring at my screen too long. One by one, my mostly silent team peeked from above their massive desktops at the oncoming chaos. I heard Calista rummaging through her drawer noisily. She suddenly stood up, holding a sharp pencil like a knife, and slid to the wall. She inched slowly towards the door at the far end.

"Calista, what are you doing?" She hushed me as if I were a three-year-old. Taken aback, I looked at my team. Peter shrugged his shoulders and went back to work, while the others looked on with a mixture of amusement and alarm. The noise from outside was getting louder. I could make out that there was another man with Drew.

"I am really calling security...damn it, this can't be happening again." Panic gripped me. Whoever it was, I couldn't let Drew deal with it alone. I rushed towards the door and promptly bumped into a hard wall of pure man. Two strong hands clutched my arms, balancing me, but I found myself bumped forward again as the full force of Calista's couple hundred pounds smashing into me. All three of us staggered back precariously, balancing ourselves. I thought I almost had it together when I heard his deep, goose bump-inducing voice.

"Careful, Nisha." My body froze, and promptly proceeded to drag all three of us onto the floor. We fell in a heap, grunts and oomphs overtaking every other noise around us. I could feel Arav's hard pecs underneath me, my hands pressing his flesh, but I felt Calista's layers of flesh above me more.

"Ow...what the hell. Someone help me up," I heard Calista grumbling as she moved off my back.

I took a deep breath of relief, my legs sliding off Arav's. I found Arav's right hand on my back, gripping my waist, softening my landing on the floor. I pushed myself off from his chest, staring at the almost-smile he had on his lips. I could kiss that smile off, but I shouldn't be thinking about that right now. Calista's grumbling grew as Drew and Peter, each holding a hand of hers, pulled her up off the floor.

"Holy mother of God, what do you eat, Cal?" Drew said, panting. I looked back at Arav, who was still staring at me, and my smile disappeared. His eyes held heat and I knew he felt the same need to touch again.

"I will help *you*, but not *him*", said Drew, his chin pointing at Arav behind me. Hands on his hips, Drew's pout looked comical. I cleared my throat. Arav sure had a way of making me speechless.

"What is your problem with Arav? And why are you always threatening to call security on him?"

"Ask him. Why is he always trying to barge in?" I looked back at Arav. He was resting himself on his elbows, his light blue shirt stretched across his chest. I struggled to keep my eyes fixed on his face. He simply shrugged and threw a challenging smile at Drew.

"He is a friend, Drew. He can come in without an appointment."

"Not when we are having a major crisis and he is the *competitor*," Drew huffed, an accusing finger pointed at Arav. That got Arav's attention, and he sat up straight.

"If I wanted to spy, I could hire the best in the field. *Barging* into my competitor's office would be a dumb way to do it."

"Whatever." Drew marched out of the corridor, pushing the glass door open with more force than necessary.

I shook my head and pushed myself off the floor. Arav was still sitting on the floor, arms around his knees. He looked far too comfortable. Before I said anything, Drew was back. He deposited five huge boxes of pizza onto the desk next to us.

"Have fun." He marched off again and I turned to Arav, wide-eyed. I would have to work really hard to make all of this up to my dear Drew.

"He hates pizza? Is that why he doesn't like me?"

"No. He is just big on drama," I said, relishing the smell of hot pizza. I couldn't remember the last time I had eaten.

"And cares too much about this company."

"Which at this moment seems unlikely to survive until tomorrow. Can we go back to fixing our problem so that we don't have to worry about our jobs?" Calista was staring at the pizza boxes as she spoke. I looked back at Arav. His face was all business now. He stood up and picked up the pizza boxes.

"Show me the way."

"Um, you can't come in." She moved in front of him, pushing me behind. "Right? This is too proprietary. Right?" I blinked as Calista's question came in focus. Of course. He was not even supposed to be aware of this crisis, let alone be in the same room where my engineers were trying to fix it.

"Is this a security breach? I can help. We had to deal with the same issue this week and I know how to fix it." He looked at me as he added softly, "That's why I couldn't be in touch this week". His absence made sense now. "I can sign a NDA if that's what is needed."

"NDA?"

"Non-disclosure agreement."

"I know what it is." I snapped, the impossible situation drawing the worst out in me. I struggled with the question. With an NDA, Arav would be bound by law to not divulge what he saw here. But he ran the company I was competing against! My goal was to surpass his company's top spot. Do arch-rivals help keep each other's companies from shutting down?

And yet, I knew I could trust Arav, even without a NDA. His moral fiber won't allow him to steal. He was too proud to win battles that way. But it was the *reason* I trusted him that made me uncomfortable.

Calista shifted on her feet, while Arav stood patiently holding the pizzas. I met his eyes, kind and reassuring. For a moment, I forgot what the issue was and why it was not a good idea to have him here. I looked away to focus on the boxes of pizza. I made my decision, and he knew my answer before I uttered it. His eyes twinkled with laughter.

"Calista, please take him to the team while I get the NDA ready." Nodding, Calista sped back to her seat, with Arav following her with the boxes of pizza. He looked back with a smile. I would never get enough of that smile.

By the time I came back with a copy of the NDA, Arav was at Peter's desk. Sleeves rolled up, his fingers were doing the dance of geekdom, while he stared at the rapidly changing black and white screen. There was something extremely sexy about geeks, and the handsome example in front of me was undoing every defense I put up against men, especially men who are a threat to my company.

Peter stood behind him, taking in every little command Arav typed in as if it were the Bible. The rest of the team was scattered, but every now and then, I found them peeking at Arav's computer, all hoping the code was cracked, and whoever hacked into our entire user base would be stopped. If they weren't not stopped immediately, we would have to announce the hack to the world, and *that* was not good news.

I found myself staring at the screen and hoping, against

my will, that Arav was able to crack the code. I walked to his desk and pulled a chair up next to him. NDA forgotten, I followed what he was trying to do. Stopping hackers midway on their way to looting data had never been my idea of fun. I recognized the code, the loop that Arav was trying to create. Peter let out a gasp. My heart raced as Arav stopped typing. The whole team gathered behind me, all eyes on the screen.

Arav's fingers hovered on the keyboard, eyes glued to the screen. He had typed in a command, pushing the hacker out of the system. We all stared at the blinking cursor, hoping it would stop moving. But we wouldn't know if it worked until the cursor started spewing out counter commands. If the hacker was still in the system, he would take control, and I could witness my company crash right in front of my eyes. I bit my cheek, trying not to scream at the screen. The tension rolled off my skin in waves. Arav didn't move an inch. His fingers were poised to type counter commands if the cursor dared to move. The cursor moved.

"Holy cow," Peter whispered, his face resembling a fish. I looked back at the screen, ready to witness the end of my company. But that wasn't what was happening. Arav was throwing commands like nobody's business. I looked at him to find a confident smile on his face. As if this was good news. As if he were winning.

I cleared my head of panic and focused on what he was typing. I dared not to make any noise when I recognized the pattern. He had not pushed the hacker out, after all. He invited him in and trapped him. The hacker had no option but to boot out. And once he was out, we would have our guards up, stronger than ever before.

Calista's loud hoot was the first indication that the hacker booted out, that we won. Adrenaline rushed through me, and I watched Arav's triumphant smile widen. But, he had no time to celebrate yet. He was typing in code to build walls all around our system. I couldn't take my eyes off him. I drank in the obsession he had with the black screen, his pure brilliance, and the passion that burned bright in his eyes. It didn't matter that he could put that brilliance to work to destroy my company. It did matter that I was up against this brilliant man, and oh, what a fight it would be!

And yet, for the first time, I wondered if I wanted to fight him. He turned to me with the same triumphant smile, and my misgiving deepened.

"I just saved your company, woman". I narrowed my eyes at him. Oh, it was so worth fighting him. I smacked the NDA in his hands.

"Sign it and hope I don't destroy yours." I could hear his laughter over all the hooting as I walked back to my office. I was glad he didn't see me smiling in return.

9

———

ARAV

"So, what now?" I pushed the signed NDA to Nisha. Her desk was filled with papers and notebooks, with a pizza box splayed open on top. If my desk were this messy, I would probably have had a headache. Yet, she seemed to thrive in this chaos.

"We eat pizza till our bellies hurt," she said, chomping a big piece of one slice. I watched her eat, relaxed against the backdrop of tall, glass NYC towers. She sat with her legs crossed on her comfortable chair. It was perfect. My sweet doe with delicate shoulders looked at home managing an empire in this big city, while unabashedly chomping down massive quantities of pizza drowning in cheese.

"I have to fit in to my suit tomorrow. So, I'll only eat one more slice," I said picking up another slice precariously, and watched as more melted cheese dripped on to the box.

"Suit? You should wear a *kurta*. It's an Indian wedding after all."

"Is that what Nikhil is going to wear?" She stopped eating mid-way and her face soured as if I spoiled the fun. I definitely liked that.

"As a matter of fact, he might. He is a stickler for dress codes and that sort of thing." She bit into her pizza again with a bit more attitude. "He is a model - rather successful, actually." I nodded. I knew all about him. I had found it impossible not to snoop into the mysterious Nikhil's background after her father mentioned him twice. I do not tell her that, of course.

"So, what happened with him?" Her body visibly sagged as she contemplated the question. She put the pizza back in her box and wiped her fingers clean with a tissue.

"It is a long story."

"We have time." I put my pizza back in the box too, giving her my full attention. She pulled her legs up, her arms holding them tight together. For the first time I wondered if I was bothering her too much by insisting.

"Well, we are childhood friends. My dad is close to his dad - the richest man in India - and it made perfect sense to have us marry. It was consolidating power." I leaned back in my chair, a finger on my lips reminding myself not to interfere. I couldn't imagine how it felt to be engaged to someone when you knew it was for convenience, and not love. "I was okay with it," she said, as if she knew what I was thinking.

Her eyes were defiant and I nodded, trying to understand her world, and how she could be okay with the arrangement. "Nikhil is a nice enough guy if you remove the fact that he has no idea how the rest of the world lives. He has always taken care of me. Sometimes, too much care," she said, her forehead creased.

Something nagged at her. Her face was clouded with mild irritation, and she unwound her legs to rest her hands and elbows on the table. "But he has absolutely no regard for my aspirations. Not his fault though. He just hasn't met a woman in his family who puts her career before men in her life. The first time I told him about Note Nirvana, he thought I looked so *cute* when I talk about my *hobbies*. I ignored it. But then he just got impatient. I needed to focus on this, but he would get mad when I wouldn't join him for his never-ending parties. And we started fighting a lot." She paused, looking away from me.

"When I refused to take Dad's money for Note Nirvana, he offered me his money, saying he couldn't wait for me to get *bored* with this and move on to more interesting hobbies." Her chin wobbled slightly, and I wanted to hug her tight. *Nice?* Nikhil seemed pretty despicable to me. "That's the day I broke up with him." I wanted to high-five her, but I restrained myself. Anger colored her cheeks slightly. "He doesn't get it though. He thinks I am just throwing a tantrum. Why don't men get the word 'no'?" I shook my head incredulously and then realized she meant men in general and that included me too.

"I always back off if a woman says no."

"Like you did when I didn't pick up your calls after you humiliated me at the coffee shop? Or the time when you barged into my office because I didn't pick up your calls?" *Oh, that.* I picked up my half-eaten pizza and stuffed my mouth with a big piece. "I thought so." She rolled her eyes and leaned back in her chair. "What bugs me the most is no one, and I mean no one objects to the way he treats me. As if...as if...it really doesn't matter what I actually dream of becoming. My role is beside him, or some other man, dutifully playing the role of a supporter, and not a doer."

She closed her eyes, sighing deeply. I watched her face, serene and defeated in that moment. She had let her defiant pose slip and bare her weakness to me. She trusted me enough to share what troubled her the most, and how powerless she felt against it. I felt privileged, but a sense of dread filled me as I realized how disappointed she must have felt in me.

I wished I could fight the battles for her. I wished I could scrub pain and disappointment out of her life so that she could fulfill all her dreams. But I was not there yet. I hadn't won her heart yet. She still held it tightly, afraid to be hurt again. Afraid to be disappointed again.

Her breathing leveled and I realized she had fallen asleep. With her hands crossed over her chest and her head leaned back in the chair, she was the rebellious princess even in sleep. But she was going to get a crick in her neck soon. I looked around to find a more comfortable spot for her to sleep on. The couch looked perfect.

I walked to her side and tapped on her shoulder lightly. Expecting her to wake up, I fluffed up the cushions on the couch, but turned back to find her in the same position on the chair. I tapped her again, but she just moved her head to the other side and continued to sleep. She snored softly, like a kitten, and I decided to record it. Okay, it was mean, but it would be my pleasure to see her blush when she watched the video the next day. Just as I ended the recording, she turned her head and sighed again. She really needed to get off that uncomfortable chair.

I debated on how to get her to the couch. The only way to do that without waking her up was to lift her off the chair. I rubbed my neck wondering if it would be the appropriate thing to do. She might be offended in the morning and I was in no mood to get another red check in her book of "reasons why I hate men so passionately".

An idea started forming in my head. I peeked out of the office only to find Calista curled up on the floor next to her desk. I cringed at the thought of waking her up. The whole team had been working like crazy all night, and I didn't have the heart to wake up anyone in the room. A big yawn escaped me, filling my eyes. I needed some sleep too if I hoped to look even half-alive at tomorrow's party.

I looked back at Nisha, her face relaxed, with no trace of the sorrow that had haunted her a few minutes back. I made my decision. I had no choice and hoped to God that I didn't fumble in my explanation tomorrow. I placed myself behind her chair and gently rolled it with Nisha on it towards the couch. She was far too deep in sleep to realize her chair was moving. I hoped that made what I was about to do next easier for. I stationed her chair to the side of the pillows on the couch and gently moved her hand off the chair's hand rest. I put one hand under her back and the other under her knees and lifted her up slightly off the chair. As I anticipated, she wasn't that heavy, but I released a heavy breath as her soft skin pressed to me. This was so not the time to think about her soft skin. I am sure she would skin me alive if she woke up now and found us like this.

I pushed the chair aside with my leg and gently deposited her on the couch. while I slipped into a kneeling position. The couch dipped as her body relaxed into it. She immediately moved, and my heart stopped. She turned on her side, her hand sliding quickly over my shoulder, freezing me on the spot. Her face was mere inches from mine, her soft breath tickling my neck. Silky black hair grazed her face, while her long eyelashes made a shadow on her cheeks. Her full lips were slightly open. Her beauty was unmarred. My fingers itched to touch her hair and withdraw the dark curtain from her face. Instead, I slowly unwrapped her hand from around my shoulder. I looked around for something to cover her with and found a throw blanket on one of the chairs.

I stepped back to see my handiwork. Satisfied that she

would now sleep much better, I left the room silently. As I tip-toed out of the office, I was startled by a loudly snoring Drew, who was passed out on the visitor's couch. I tried to move as quietly as possible, but I heard him wake up with a jolt at the sound of the elevator.

"She is alive, I promise". I said, hands in the air.

"I will deal with you tomorrow. I promise." His eyes drooped closed. I chuckled alone in the elevator. I had to win over Drew if I had any chance of winning over Nisha.

I BLINKED RAPIDLY, trying to drive away the lingering sleep. Nisha's home looked dreary today, creating pale shadows in the grey, overcast weather. Being sleep-ridden wasn't helping to brighten up the outlook. The only real bright spot was the fact that I would actually get to see Nisha.

I shifted in the overly comfortable lounge chair in the formal living room and checked my watch for the umpteenth time. It was eight-thirty, making me thirty minutes early, despite reaching my home at three in the morning. After just about three hours of sleep, I had to rush to my uncle's place in Queens to pick up my *sherwani*. I also boxed up three more *kurtas* to take home, in case of emergency traditional dates like the one today.

I pressed the back of my palms on to my eyes and sighed. It felt good to keep my eyes closed, even for a few seconds. This had been a week on steroids, with multiple cyber-attacks at TechNotes. While we successfully squashed them, the fact that the hackers were now on to Note Nirvana only means they were not letting up anytime soon. I had left a note for Peter to keep a close watch before I left in the morning.

And then, there was Nisha. Every second I had to myself, she was on my mind. Her business drive and her personal vulnerability were contradictory, in an intriguing and tempting way. No amount of research could have prepared me for the sweet girl inside the successful startup founder. She was not ready for this marriage, though. Actually, she was not ready for any relationship. She was too worried about being shadowed by the men in her life. Who could blame her? I had seen my mother's struggles firsthand.

Considering how our companies were rivals, I didn't doubt her fears. The worst part was I didn't have a plan. Smart as I was, I didn't have a single clue as to how to keep our companies separate and still convince Nisha to say yes to our marriage. The fact that her company was inching in on us didn't help at all. My protective instincts to save my company had kicked in time and again, and I had become a full-throttle mama bear at work.

And yet, switching mama bear mode off was so easy when I was with Nisha. When I looked at her, I didn't see a competitor. I saw a beautiful, kind woman who I would like to spend my life with. I wondered what she saw in me, if anything. So far, all I got was reluctance about the whole marriage idea, and not to mention, a general hatred for my species.

I rubbed my face, brushed my hair with my fingers and checked the time again. Twenty-five minutes more to go. I probably should have napped in the car for few minutes instead of waiting in here and announcing my desperation to the world. I was just about to walk back to my car when I heard heavy footsteps. I turned back to find Kamlesh Jain striding towards me with a slight smile. Dressed in ethnic clothes, his demeanor seemed softer - almost fatherly.

"Right on time again. How are you doing, Arav?" I shook

his hand while he patted my back. Considering how tense the last time I met him was, this was quite a change. "Nisha mentioned at breakfast that you had helped her out yesterday with a crisis. I hope she thanked you for it. She is not very good at taking help."

"She made me sign a NDA, sir." His boisterous laugh bounced in the huge room.

"Have fun today. I will meet you at the wedding later," he called out as he walked away from me.

I stood staring at the empty door where Kamlesh Jain left. Two assistants followed him with iPads tucked under their arms. A smile tugged at my face as I realized something. For all the fire my little dragon spewed, she was surrounded by people who would maul me alive if I hurt her. That ought to have been a warning, but it only made me feel prouder of her.

Sounds of jingling anklets drew my attention, and I turned around to see Nisha descending the stairs. My heart skipped a beat at the vision before me. She was dressed in an orange *lehenga choli* - a long skirt and matching blouse embellished with tiny mirrors and beads – and her long, shimmering *dupatta* wrapped around her body like water. Her raven-black hair was left loose, and it framed her face with the darkness of night, giving it a moonlit glow. She smiled at me, and her eyes told me she noticed my ethnic wear, too. I smiled back, curling my hands into fists to make sure I didn't reach out to her. I walked toward her as she descended the steps, offering my arm.

"*Sherwani* suits you. You clean up fast . . . and well, Arav," she said, apprising my dark blue knee-length coat.

"Comes quite handy in crushing competition." Her eyes sparkled at my taunt.

"Then you need to improve your game. I foresee your winning streak coming to an end."

"If it were for a pretty lady like you, I might trade in for a loss." Color rose in her cheeks and I didn't miss a second of it. "Did you sleep well?"

"As a matter of fact, yes. The couch was quite comfy. Thank you." Her voice soft, she sounded earnest and not the least bit annoyed, as I had imagined. I shrugged, looking as casual as I could. She smiled at me, our eyes meeting for the first time. That was when I felt it again, a live, buzzing connection with her that I felt so strongly the first time we met. I couldn't take my eyes off her. She averted her gaze and started adjusting her *dupatta*. And just like that, I lost the connection. Her fingers shook a little as she set the folds of her long scarf over her arms. I looked away from her, breathing in her light scent from the air. Apparently, the moment had passed. I slid my hands in the pockets, the car keys reminding me of the journey we had to take in a few moments.

"We should leave now-"

"You should get some coffee-"

"Sure, coffee's good-"

"Yes, we don't want to be late-" She laughed out loud, her bangles jingling as she pushed her long hair over her arm. I stepped closer, my fingers itching to touch her. She was still smiling when I took a wayward lock of hair that was caressing her cheeks and tucked it behind her ears. The softness of her ear tickled, my fingers lingering there. She had stopped smiling, her eyes meeting mine with a tenderness I had not witnessed before. My gazed moved to her lips, tinted with a beautiful dark peach. She let out a soft sigh. "I think we should leave now...unless you want some coffee," she said. I nodded, trying to get my head out of the clouds. I was better than this. Never had any woman had me this out of control.

"Let's go," I said taking a step back. *Before I do something stupid.*

She walked in front of me, her *lehenga* swaying with her, her anklets and bangles creating harmonious music. I could listen to that soft jingling all day. Her laughter only added to the orchestra. Every trace of my sleepiness was gone, and I found myself looking forward to spending the whole day with her.

"THAT'S SHEILA AND AMIT," said Nisha nodding at a well-dressed couple at the other end of the garden. "If you meet them, compliment Sheila's jewelry. They own a jewelry chain in the city." I nodded, taking a sip of the fresh Rose Sharbet "And that's Diana and Kalki. Don't compliment them and use words sparsely." She looked up at me, sensing my confusion. "They are page three reporters. Everything is news. And you and I?," she added wagging a finger between us, "We would be their hefty annual bonus."

"Got it. Stay away from D&K co." She snickered at my attempt at humor while I checked out the gathering as I lounged on a bar stool under one of the mini-bars.

The wedding venue was none other than the bride's gigantic *backyard*. It turned out Priya, the bride, was Nisha's childhood friend, and she was marrying Sean, another childhood friend of hers. They all grew up together, which meant Nikhil was part of this story in a big way. It seemed like marrying childhood sweethearts was a tradition in this group.

A few of Nisha's friends were already tut-tutting at the

news of her break up with Nikhil. Clearly, I was not going to be very popular here. Not that I cared, because Nisha seemed to take extra pleasure in introducing me to everyone as her date, and that meant more to me than making a good impression on strangers.

I gazed at the growing crowd. They were finely clothed, and richness floated graciously in the beautifully decorated garden. Flower garlands hung from the trees, and shiny, golden ribbons swirled around the trunks, giving it a fairy tale look. Numerous waiters, dressed in white, handed out sharbets to the guests. Considering the hot day, the cool flavored fruit drink was definitely a good choice. It was a well-arranged event, though hardly the kind of place I would be at voluntarily. I preferred the cold walls of my office.

And yet, here I was accompanying Nisha as her *date,* when we both knew it was anything but. I was hoping our date the day before would help us get to know each other better, but, thanks to the hacker sitting somewhere in Eastern Europe, a well-planned date at one of the best restaurants in Manhattan turned to a pizza party at her office. Not that I regretted it. At least I was able to spend some time with her.

Tomorrow. I would ask her if she was available tomorrow so that I could take her on a date.

"Nikhil," she whispered, elbowing me on the side softly. She tensed up next to me, her expression bereft of the laughter it held just a few moments before. I looked up to find an extremely good-looking man who was almost as tall as me walking towards us. He didn't look happy, but he wore a smile that could easily pass as cordial.

"Hey," he said, and taking her in a tight embrace. My grip on my cup tightened as I watched Nisha in his arms - a hug that took longer than necessary. Nisha finally broke the embrace and took a step back, creating space between them, but Nikhil took a step closer, cupping her face. "I missed you," he said and before I knew what was happening, he dipped to kiss her lips.

I jumped from my seat, my hands in fists at my side, ready to punch him if need be. But Nisha had already turned her face towards me, so his lips landed on her cheek. She looked up, mild amusement in her eyes. I felt hot rage, but the way she looked at me, as though chiding me for overreacting, helped me relax. I reminded myself that she was fully capable of handling Nikhil by herself.

I walked over and stood calmly by her side. I was still looking at Nisha when Nikhil cleared his throat. I looked up to find him giving ups a disgusted glare, as though he saw filth flying around.

"Hi, I'm Arav Shetty. Nice to meet you. And you are?" I asked as he shook my hand.

"Nikhil Verma. Surely she has mentioned me, considering you are here." His eyes shot daggers at me.

"Not really. We have been busy with other things." She opened her mouth in astonishment, then swallowed and smiled nervously.

"Well yeah...quite busy, I must say." Nikhil huffed audibly. She shook her head at him, then smiled at me. The chiding look was long gone - replaced with a mischievous spark. Still gazing at me, she said "Nikhil, meet Arav, my date, and . . . my fiancé." It was my turn to gape at her. Her smile grew bigger, challenging me to correct the information, but why would I? It sounded perfect, even if it was a lie.

"Excuse me?" Eyes bulging out, Nikhil didn't look as well as he did before. He shifted on his feet, anger coming off him in rolls. "Kamlesh uncle said nothing about this to me."

He wasn't even glancing at me anymore. His full attention was on Nisha, as he tried to intimidate her.

I reached out for her hand and pressed it gently. I sensed she was about to push the fake engagement ploy a little further. I nodded slightly in encouragement.

Nisha straightened, meeting Nikhil's stern gaze. "It's not official yet. I haven't told Dad about my decision." He snickered his pretty face no longer looking so pretty.

"It has never been your decision."

"Well, it is now. Get used to it." She crossed her hands. I stepped forward, shoulder to shoulder with Nisha, facing Nikhil. People had started giving us furtive glances, and I hoped Nikhil's theatrics would die down soon.

"We will see about that," said Nikhil, nodding towards Nisha. "And you, Mr. Arav Shetty - don't get too comfortable around here. She is known for her impulsive bad decisions."

I heard her gasp softly as she watched Nikhil stomp away. I pulled her closer, weaving my arm around her shoulder, and I gently kissed her hair. She relaxed, her hand tugging my *sherwani* as she turned to me slightly. Nikhil had left us to deal with murmurs of the drama around us alone. We stood there in a half-embrace. I felt her humiliation, and hurt was evident in her face.

"Next time he speaks to you that way, I think you should be as brutal to him as you were to me."

She looked up at me, her eyebrows knit. Her doe-eyes were clouded with defeat. "Shut him up. Kill all communication. Scoop his eyes out with a spoon." She rolled her eyes and pushed me away gently. Settling herself on the bar stool, she took a *sharbet* from the passing waiter.

"I didn't scoop your eyes out." She said flatly and took a sip. I sat next to her, picking up my *sharbet* from the bar.

"No. You scooped my heart out." I turned to find her

watching me, a quiet gaze that reflected my own thoughts. *How far have we come in just a week?* From arch-rivals to fake fiancés. What else was in store for us? We were interrupted by peals of laughter from just outside the garden entryway. The laughter was followed by the full resonance of many *dholaks* - two-headed drums played together by men dressed in bright orange and yellow garments.

With the sudden rush of guests towards the procession, I realized the groom's family had arrived, and the traditional *baraat* procession had begun. The procession began with kids, teens, and the *dholak* players walking - or rather dancing their way towards the enormous stage that was specially built for the bride and the groom. The bride's family was waiting at the base of the stage with *tilak*, the red-colored spots to be worn on the forehead by all the guests. I heard the sweet rustling of Nisha's *lehenga* as she stood up and started adjusting her *dupatta*.

"What are you doing?" She tucked one end of the dupatta at her waist, trapping it beneath so that it didn't slip off or blow away.

"Come on, time to move that cute tushy for the groom." She took my hand and started walking towards the procession.

"But, I thought we were the bride's guests?" She shook her head, her laughter drowned out by the loud music around us.

"We represent both. We dance in the *baraat* as part of groom's family, and then we serve the groom's family as our guests. Now don't ask more questions." She turned around, shaking her shoulder as she joined the group of increasingly rowdy dancers and added, "I can't hear you, anyway."

The cacophony of laughter, greetings and just plain, old-fashioned squeals of happiness were infectious as we danced with the *baraatis*. Nisha had transformed in this group, hugging her friends, moving her feet and arms in rhythm with the invigorating beats of the *dhoakl*. She pulled me towards her, her face aglow with unbridled laughter. We moved in tandem, right foot for right, left arm for left, her long *lehenga* skirt brushing my feet as she twirled. Her dark hair moved like waves, draping her arms.

"You have been keeping secrets," I whispered into her ear, pulling her close. She tilted her head up, shocked at the sudden touching of our bodies. "Your dancing skills are quite a revelation." I felt her shiver as my lips touched her ears. She pushed me back with her hands, moving in rhythm.

"You are not so bad yourself." She joined another woman, who was dressed in a blue *lehenga* and quickly formed a circle with other women around. She looked back once and smiled, her cheeks flushed. The women around her held hands, forming a tight little circle. Then they danced together, moving in and out of the circle like a flower blooming in the morning dew.

I looked around for Nikhil, but he was nowhere to be found. We were at the center of the noisy crowd, mingling with guests of all ages. Their rich, colorful clothes shimmered in the morning light as they danced their hearts out in honor of the bride and groom. As soon as the procession reached the base of the stage, where the bride's family waited to welcome each of us with a *tilak* and a garland, I felt Nisha tug me out of the crowd. We rushed to stand right behind the welcoming bride's family. Nisha thrust a few flower garlands in my hands to hold while she presented them to the oncoming guests.

The music was blaring its loudest when I finally got a glimpse of the groom. He was alighting from a flower-adorned Bentley, dressed in a velvet maroon *sherwani* and a beige silk turban. Nisha rushed to meet him, hugging him tight while he lifted her up off the ground. Someone teased that he was cheating on the bride, and the laughter in the crowd reached a deafening level. He put Nisha down and she walked back to stand next to me. She entwined her fingers in mine. I wasn't even sure she realized she was holding my hand. I gazed at her flushed face. She was happy. This was the real her. I pressed her hand slightly to remind myself that this was real. That this beautiful, kind-hearted, lioness was real. She looked at me, her eyes alight. In that instant, I knew I was in love with her. I loved her enough to be her fake fiancé, and I loved her enough to wait until she agreed to marry me for real.

But a sudden realization hit me. Nothing mattered until she loved me - all of me. There were still many things about my past that I hadn't told her. What would she think when she found out about my abusive father? Any sane woman would fear a repetition of history. Nisha was not only sane, but extremely smart. Would I lose her before I even had her?

Doubt crept in, and my grip on her hand loosened. In the midst of the blaring music and the wedding shenani-gans, I felt my heart constrict with the pain of losing Nisha. I needed to tell her everything as soon as I could. Maybe she would understand, just like her father did. Maybe I could prove to her that I was nothing like my father. I was so engrossed in my thoughts that I didn't realize that Nisha was looking at me oddly.

"Are you okay?" She waved her hand in front of my face. I blinked. Though the laughter had dimmed, and the crowd had dispersed around the wedding stage, her pretty face was still there. I rubbed my face and let out a sigh.

"Will you come on a date with me tomorrow, please?" At this point, I was ready to get on my knees and beg. I was grateful it hadn't come to that yet. Brows knitted, she bit her lip.

"Tomorrow is-"

"Please. We need time together to move past fake fiancés and think about a real engagement." At that, her eyebrows shot up.

"Who said I want to make this real?" My heart thudded to a skid. *What?* "God, I was kidding!" she exclaimed. "Look at your face. You look pale as death!" She picked a cup of water from a nearby waiter and handed it to me. "Drink up. What's up with you today, Arav? You are acting really weird." I rubbed the back of my neck, relieving some stress. With arms crossed, she watched as I drank up the water. The cool beverage felt refreshing. I let out a sigh. It was time to come clean.

"Nisha, I think I am in-"

"So, fiancé huh?" We turned at the same time to find Nikhil standing with his arms crossed.

Nisha instantly tensed next to me. A small crowd of about four men had formed behind Nikhil. From the picture-perfect looks of each, I guessed they were his friends. "I just got off the phone with your father," he said, looking directly at Nisha, "And do you know what he said about you making a decision?" Nisha pulled up her chin, facing him eye to eye. "That he doesn't mind your fancy start-up games, but you'd better leave important decisions to him. And by important, he means not getting attached to ..." he tilted his head slightly towards me and said, "roaches like him."

"Mind your language, Nikhil. This is no way to talk to our guests." All of Nisha's light-heartedness had disappeared. Nikhil stepped closer to us. I knew he wouldn't harm her, but I angled my body slightly, enclosing her in my private space.

"He..." His gaze was full of contempt. "...is not up to any kind of standard to be our guest." Nisha's face flushed with anger.

"Enough of your empire crap, Nikhil. If you are talking about money, he has more than all of your friends combined. Now lay off." She seethed with anger, her shoulders rising and falling with her heavy breathing. But Nikhil only smirked. I had a feeling I knew where this was going.

"Not if he is a woman-beater." Nisha gasped. She took a step back, shoulder to shoulder with me. My heart thudded in my chest. This was not the way I wanted Nisha to hear about this. I could have killed Nikhil right there, but then it would only prove his point. "It looks like he hasn't enlightened you about the fine print that comes with being Arav Shetty's woman. While our families take pride in building an empire of successful companies, his...well, let's just say his have built an empire of police complaints. That's *his* legacy."

"Did my father tell you that?" The silence in her voice was unnerving.

"No. It took me less than thirty minutes to find it out myself." My hands in fists, I struggled to keep my breathing even. Nisha deserved better than this. I turned to her, expecting her to be disgusted, but instead she was staring at me with an unreadable expression. Then, she quietly pried my fist open and slipped her hand in mine. I relaxed a bit, overcome with relief that all was not lost. She had given me the benefit of the doubt and that was all I needed. Maybe I would have a chance to explain.

But Nikhil was clearly not done. Tension was crept up

into my neck again. "Are you really this stupid? Did you bother looking him up before rushing to sleep with him?"

"Wow, so money really doesn't breed class." I stepped forward, pushing Nisha behind me. "If you are done with showing everyone what a spineless pig you are, we have better things to do." I stood face to face with Nikhil. I had been wrong about one thing. I definitely stood taller than him, and despite the muscle I could see stretching under his Sherwani, I knew I he was no match for me. It would take one sudden punch to stun him. I wondered what his pretty face would look like after my fist connected with his nose.

Nisha's soft hand on my shoulder startled me. Tension had roiled my muscles tight. Nikhil, to his credit, had not moved an inch, but he was also had four of his friends behind him. Jaw clenched tight, I looked behind me at Nisha and she silently shook her head. I turned to Nikhil, waiting for his next step.

He stepped closer and said in a loud whisper, "You do know that she has spent a great number of years warming my bed, right?"

The next moments were a blur. I remember my knuckles meeting the sharp bone of his nose, and the sickening sound of as it cracked, but after that, it was all meaningless chaos. Nikhil fell back on his friends while blood sputtered from his nose. Nisha rushed to me, watching in horror as Nikhil's friends held his silk scarf over his face in an attempt to stop the bleeding. Her hands found mine again and she held them tight as if her life depended on it. Surprisingly, no one thought of tackling me and I just stood there, rubbing my knuckles while people around us rushed to his aid.

An elderly gentleman in a silk brown kurta ushered Nisha and I away from the crowd and we followed silently. Nisha clutched my hand the whole time, and as we headed urgently to the parking space, she tightened her hold and tugged at me, urging me to walk faster. Wedding guests looked back as we hurried down to the parking lot to the car. As we reached the parking lot, Nisha stopped and turned to the man escorting us.

"Thank you Siddharth uncle. I am so sorry about this. I didn't mean to make a scene at Priya's wedding." I realized the man escorting us out was none other than the bride's father. I felt incredibly guilty. He patted her gently.

"I am glad this young man here stood up for you. I didn't expect this from Nikhil." He then looked at me, his eyes appraising me from head to toe. "Kamlesh has spoken to me about you." He paused, his forehead creased. "I watched you drink the poison of your father's sin silently, but you couldn't take one word against Nisha. I would tell Kamlesh that he has found a gem for his daughter," he turned to Nisha before he added, "if she agrees to accept you." I could see the indecision in her eyes and I lowered mine and took a deep breath.

"Nisha is free to reject me but that still doesn't justify Nikhil's words. I would gladly do it again if needed." I said the words with utmost sincerity, but Siddharth's eyes had softened and he let out a low chuckle.

"I assure you it won't be needed. Good luck to you both and Nisha," he kissed her forehead and said, "I will tell Priya that you had to leave. Don't worry about upsetting her. We will meet tomorrow at the reception party." He left us with a pat on my arm. I fished the keys of my Audi out of my pocket, my sore knuckles grazing the rough fabric of my *Sherwani*. No regrets. We got into the car and drove out of the busy parking lot in silence. This was not how the day was supposed to go. Not at all.

10

NISHA

W ow. Just wow. I had imagined this day so differently. I would finally get to relax. I would introduce Arav to my friends. I would get to enjoy Priya's wedding and Arav's company - not necessarily in that order.

It had all started off well enough. When I woke up on my couch at work, I knew it was Arav who was thoughtful enough to move me there. Judging by the distance from my chair to the couch, I realized he had put in a lot of thought into how to transfer me there. My face heated up at the thought, and I giggled like a little girl.

I had rushed home, determined not to be late, but Arav was almost a half an hour early. It must have taken him a while to reach home from my office, so I couldn't imagine that he had gotten enough sleep.

I was excited. Butterflies created havoc in my belly. I had expected to find Arav all suited up for the wedding, but I was wrong. He surprised me with his traditional attire, and stole my breath with just a smile. His dark blue *sherwani* and beige *chudidar* pants accentuated his athletic figure, while the color complimented his tanned skin tone. The butter-flies went wild, and my heart beat faster. I found myself looking forward to the full day I would spend in his company, listening to the rich baritone of his voice.

I had anticipated Nikhil to spoil some of the fun, but I didn't imagine the hatred in his eyes when he finally realized he was rejected. To be honest, I was scared. It was terrifying to have Nikhil stand so close to me and tell me this marriage was not really my decision. I hated him for saying that - for claiming I wasn't good enough to make my own decisions. Somewhere deep down, I think I believed it too. My heart hurt at his cruelty, but the pain stopped the moment I felt Arav's hand in mine.

Arav's eyes held strength - the kind of assurance I had been seeking from everyone around me, but never found. I had charged through my business when no one had faith in me. I hadn't needed their faith to be successful, but having it mattered to me. I didn't know how much it mattered until Arav gave me his faith unconditionally.

I felt strangely light-hearted afterwards, my mind resting from the unrelenting questions that had plagued it. I was able to just enjoy the immense pleasure of being with a strong man who wasn't afraid to let a woman race ahead of him. Even though he had never promised me his protection. I felt safe and secure with him.

Therefore, when Nikhil pronounced him a woman-beater, I flinched as if flogged a thousand times. Was Arav capable of such a thing? I had felt him tense up next to me. Not the way a thief tenses up after getting caught, but the way a man who was running short on time to prove himself might. In that instant, I decided Nikhil would not define Arav for me. I would let Arav speak for himself. It might be ugly, and he very well might turn out to be exactly what

Nikhil said he was - as incomprehensible as that was to me - but it was his story to tell.

You'd think Arav pounding his fist into Nikhil's nose would give Nikhil's claims more credibility, but the moron deserved that and more. If I had had the chance to add my own fist to his nose . . . if only –

"I'm sorry." I jumped in my seat, startled by Arav's sudden apology. I released the hand rest that I had been unconsciously mauling with my hand.

The silence in the car felt heavy as his apology sat hanging in the air. I shook my head, clearing memories of the muddled morning.

"Don't be." I cleared my throat. "And thank you...for defending me." He faced ahead, his jaw clenched. His grip on the steering wheel was tight enough to whiten his knuckles. The bruises there showed some color already.

I studied his profile in silence. His slightly curled hair was ruffled from the fight. With his lips pursed and his skin tight with tension, his face looked stern. But even his anger couldn't mask the kindness he had shown me back there when he decided to teach Nikhil some manners.

Siddharth uncle was right - his own humiliation didn't move him at all but mine did. I looked out at the colorful trees zooming past us and wondered why I was still undecided. In his presence, I found myself forgetting the reasons why I didn't want to marry him. I almost forgot how my whole identity was threatened to be overshadowed by his. I forgot how I would be reduced to nothing but the arm candy that rich men needed.

When I looked back at him again, his face had relaxed a bit. He smiled at me, the kind of smile that brought the butterflies all out in force. I sighed in defeat. Now was not the time to debate marrying Arav. Right now, I just wanted to be home. I watched the Hudson River ripple strongly beneath us as we crossed the Palisades Interstate Parkway towards George Washington Bridge and entered Manhattan. Once we touched the bridge, we would be back to the chaos of New York City, and of my mind. I wanted to go home, to spend a few minutes of peace away from the chaos we had left behind.

Fall colors dominated the thick vegetation on the side of the parkway. Nestled in the midst of the trees was my *real* home, a hideout no one knew about. I longed to be there and experience the peace and quiet of nature, but could I share my secret with Arav? I turned back to find him looking at me with concern.

"Are you feeling okay about going home now? Do you want some time for yourself?" I almost whimpered with relief. He could read me like an open book. That should have bothered me, but right then I was just glad that he recognized my need to take a break from the freaking world. I shook my head.

"Can I enter an address in your GPS? I would rather go there for few hours before heading home." Amused, he nodded, and I punched the address.

My home was nestled deep within the greenery lining the Hudson River, in Englewood Cliffs, New Jersey. I bought it with my first bonus from Note Nirvana a year before. I had always found the skyline view of New York City from the New Jersey side of the Hudson river mesmerizing. So, when I found a listing for a one-bedroom cottage on the rock, I bought it without a second thought. It was my refuge from the world - my one safe place when my family, the company, the world was too much to bear. This was one of those times, but today I didn't want to be alone. I wanted to share my safe haven with Arav. He understood my struggle, and it seemed as though he spent some moments of his life in the same hell that I did.

"Where are we going?" he asked, as he made a U-turn on the I-95.

"You will see." As we weaved into the rough, trail-like street leading into the vegetation, Arav looked at me suspiciously.

"Do you plan to push me into the Hudson River for ruining your friend's wedding?"

"By the time I am done with you, you will wish I did that instead." His chest rose and fell enticingly as he laughed. I rested my head on the plush seat smiling. It felt good to share my life's biggest secret with him.

We stopped at a cottage. About half of the walls featured half-log wooden siding, and about half were built with floor-to-ceiling glass. The whole house was the perfect mix of warm classic architecture and reliable modern technology. Not so when I bought it. The cottage itself was over sixty years old. It was built well enough to last another sixty with ease, but it was old enough to lack any modern amenities. I hired an architect friend to make it modern enough for my taste, and she transformed it to something that I lovingly called home.

I stared at the huge oak door that I had added, admiring its rich warm color. I got out of the car and waited for Arav to park.

"I wish I was dressed for this getaway," he said, looking down at his *sherwani.* I was dressed no better in my *lehenga,* but I had clothes to change into.

We walked to the front porch together. I pulled open a small cover on the side of the door that hid a fingerprint lock. I scanned my thumb in and entered the code. The door clicked, and I pushed it open. Arav looked impressed, and I congratulated myself. This place was secluded enough to give security some serious thought, and my friend had done an excellent job with it.

We entered into the living room, which had warm, dark oak flooring, and was large enough to fit a L sectional with a center table. I had minimal furniture in the room - only the necessities. No clutter to worry about; just peace of mind. The house was spotless, exactly the way I had left it. Arav walked ahead of me into the open kitchen, an oasis of white cabinets and marble countertops. It was lined with the most modern appliances available on the market. My friend had hooked me up with the best interior designer in her firm, and she had outdone herself with her selections.

"Impressive," he said as he fished for a cup in the cabinets. He poured himself a glass of water from the fridge and gulped it down.

"I told my friend to equip it with everything I would need to live like a hermit. She did exactly that. I can live here for a week without seeing another human. Isn't that wonderful?" I stood resting my palms on the kitchen island. Arav looked thoughtful, with the water glass still in his hands.

"Why would you not want to see another human?" I shrugged and opened the freezer to pull out some ready-to-eat pouches of pasta and noodles.

"Hungry?"

He looked at my selection of frozen items.

"That one. Pepperoni pizza heals everything. Including this," he said pointing at his knuckles. I raised my eyebrows at the swollen knuckles.

"I think you need to wash that off first. I will get a bandage for you." I said, as I put the frozen pizza in the oven. I paused in thought. "He's going to call the cops on you." I faced the oven, suddenly feeling guilty - and worried for Arav. Nikhil seemed borderline crazy, refusing to give up on our relationship. It will be all over the press if cops get involved.

I heard running water in the sink, and I watched Arav wash his hand, seemingly lost in thought. I was sure he was thinking the same as me. Media attention for the wrong reasons could wreak havoc on companies these days, inviting scrutiny in a way with no parallel in history. With a dark family past like his, he already carried a heavy burden.

I walked away, giving him some space to process while I changed into something more comfortable. Life was simple in my one-bedroom cottage. My friend had managed to squeeze a small walk in closet into the design, and I found myself rummaging through clothes that were none too appealing, like my ten-year-old ratty T-shirts. But that was all I found, so I decided to put on a pair of tights and a loose white V-neck that was extremely soft, thanks to the thousand washes it had gone through. I quickly freshened up, removing my make-up and bunching my hair up into a messy bun. I finally felt fresh and relaxed.

I returned to the kitchen to find Arav on the bar stool at the kitchen island, scrolling through something on his phone. Hot pizza was ready on the island.

"You want me to wear this?" He gingerly picked up the black *Note Nirvana* company hoodie I pushed towards him on the island. I nodded, relishing the incredulous look on his face.

"You are in luck. I found some company swag in the closet. The hoodie is unisex. Also, here is a pair of active pants. Hopefully they will fit." I took a bite from the slice of pizza I pulled, while he made disgusted faces.

"This is how you repay me for defending your honor." I snickered.

"I never asked for it, my shining knight in *sherwani*." He shrugged and proceeded to unbutton. My throat dried up and I averted my gaze. It was hard not to look at the mesmerizing golden skin on his chest as he unbuttoned. I sneaked in a peek and I caught him staring at me with a smug smile.

"Are you going to change right here?" I cleared my throat, inwardly cringing at how hoarse I sounded.

"Do you want me to?" I squirmed in my seat under his attentive gaze. There was mischief and heat in his eyes, I looked away once again.

"Bathroom's that way," I said pointing to the bedroom. I squirmed again. He would be entering my "safe place." No one had set foot in there, but now he would see my refuge from the world. The alarming part was I wasn't afraid to show it to him.

11

ARAV

If there was one thing I was sure of, is that Nisha Jain would be the death of me. With just one sweet glance, she could walk me off the edge of a cliff. Or parade me throughout Manhattan wearing a Note Nirvana hoodie. I slipped the hoodie over my head, cursing softly. If Ryan saw me with this on, he would disown me this very instant. How did I get here?

I smirked recalling my first meeting with Nisha, when I presented my cocky self, assuming the cake walk buying this company would be. I sighed, examining myself in the only full-length mirror that I found, which was in her walk-in closet. I hated to admit the hoodie looked good on me. The active pants, on the other hand, were too loose. I secured them with the drawstring. Facing the mirror, I took a moment to appreciate where I was standing.

I was in Nisha's closet, in her secret hideout, surrounded by - scratch that - overwhelmed by her lingering smell. It was hard to think straight, but I was still able to recognize what a big step this was for her. She willingly let me enter her inner sanctum, and I was grateful for her trust in me.

She was usually overly cautious with me, and seeing how Nikhil had treated her earlier, I was not surprised.

I brushed my messy hair back with my fingers, hoping to tame it enough to look somewhat tidy. The sight of my wounded knuckles brought the whole unpleasant Nikhil affair back. The cold water had helped with the swelling, but the redness remained. The cream should help it to heal faster.

I hadn't been in a fight since high school. It used to upset my mom immensely if I came home with a bruise, and it never mattered who started the fight. I was not supposed to fight. Period. I think she had a terrible fear that I would turn into my father, but she had no idea that the very idea was a nightmare to me. I would never be my father.

As I grew older, I realized some of my mother's fear was legitimate. There was one thing I did get from my father - his famed short temper. So, I learned to keep myself calm, even in infuriating situations. Like Nikhil thinking it was fair game to claim wife-beating was my legacy. I worked unbelievably hard to ensure that my father's past was erased from public memory. But it was okay. I had learned to deal with jealous knuckleheads like that.

But how do you stay quiet when the woman you love was humiliated in the worst possible way? How do you not punch the crap out of a man who dares to suggest that she was nothing but a whore? Anger pulsed through me once again. I saw red every time I recalled the pleasure I saw in his eyes as he demeaned the very woman he wanted to marry. I wonder what else Nisha had put up with. I took a deep cleansing breath and walked out of the room.

I found Nisha nibbling at a slice of pizza. When she saw me, she pushed a plate with two slices onto my side of the island and I settled in to finally take a deeply satisfying bite.

I almost moaned in pleasure as I bit into the soft bread layered with about a half a pound of cheese. After the previous adrenaline rush, my body was demanding food to keep going. My phone buzzed again and I muted it. It was Ryan calling for the third time. I texted him a brief summary of what happened and asked him to watch out for any media attention. Of course, it was too juicy a story for him not to demand more details, but I was not ready to face Ryan - or the rest of the world – just yet.

"This is a pretty neat place. Amazing view." I looked out at the NYC skyline from the huge glass walls in her living room. It was mesmerizing to watch the Hudson River kiss the banks of a city that refused to stop moving. The water seemed to offer a few moments of peace and calm to the people living these unstoppable lives. Nisha nodded as her gaze followed the city's quickly darkening horizon.

"No one knows about this house. I bought it a year and a half ago. It was a treat to myself, for..." Her smile dimmed, and her eyes shimmered with unshed tears. She blinked rapidly and took a deep, shuddering breath.

"For being so brave. For achieving your dreams...alone." Our eyes met, and for an instant I felt she wanted to say more, but after a moment's hesitation, she looked away.

"You know too much about me. Tell me your story." She took another bite of her pizza and pushed the plate away.

"The typical story of an immigrant. My mother sent me here hoping I would have a better future. I lived with my maternal uncle and grew up dreaming of building my own business. Which I did, and I am very proud of. End of story." I knew I said it too quickly. It wasn't hard for her to pick up on the hidden context behind this vanilla version.

"Tell me something that I don't know about the story." She sat with her elbows on the island, head tilted slightly in full attention. I realized that this was her first real attempt at knowing me better - asking me for something more than what I readily offered.

"The last time I was in a fight, my mom borrowed money from my grandfather to book a one-way ticket to the USA." She blinked, her mouth sucking a quick gasp. "I didn't fight a lot, but I did get into trouble. My mother was terrified that-"

"-you would turn into your father." Anger simmered under my skin at her words. It was irrational to feel this burn in my veins at the mere mention of the possibility. I took a calming breath and looked away. I felt her hand on mine and her soft gaze felt like an embrace. She had a sympathetic and compassionate smile.

"Every day that I don't get into a fight - that I fight my battles the civilized way - I prove to the world I am not my father." She squeezed my hand lightly. I held her hand, caressing her knuckles, the slender fingers. "I loved my mother more than anyone in the world. He was not kind to her. I watched her suffer. I would not wish that on any woman. If you fear I would-"

"I don't. I don't believe that is your legacy, Arav. You are not a coward. You would never hit a woman. I know that in my heart." I released a relieved breath that I didn't realize I was holding. I swallowed, my hands holding on to her for dear life. I wanted to hug her so tight, tell her how much I loved her in that instant, and how I was falling irrevocably more in love with her with every passing minute. Yet, I could sense her hesitation.

"Are you willing to give us a chance?" I felt bereft as she gently removed her hand from mine.

"You are a very successful man, Arav."

"Is that a bad thing?"

"My biggest fear is that I will turn into my mother." I angled my head and watched as she pushed the loose strands of hair off her face. I had never heard much about her mother, except that Nisha lost her to cancer when she was young.

She wet her lips. "Did you know she graduated top of her class in business administration from NYU Stern?" I shook my head, wondering where this was going. "Everyone saw a bright future for her. She did have one, according to many. She married my father, the up-and-coming real estate magnate." Shoulders sagging and head bent, she chipped at her nail polish. "She was depressed most of her married life. I think...embracing death at the end was easy for her."

We sat in silence. I set my pizza down, hunger long gone. I thought back to any references I had heard to her mother since I met her. There were none, except for the one time her father mentioned her. He sounded fond of his late wife, but that was it. There was nothing more to it.

She walked towards the front door, picking up a throw on the couch on her way. Crisp, cold fall air seeped in as she opened the huge oak door and settled on the front porch stairs. She let out a shudder as she bundled herself in the throw blanket.

Her cottage indeed had one the best views of New York. Trees were cleared out in the small patch of land in front of her house. The sound of rushing river dominated the air around us, while the twinkling skyline of the city stood witness to the magnificent capability of humans to build dreams and succeed. Nisha's cottage must have cost a small fortune. A small well of pride surged within me. This was what I loved the most about her - her ability to make it on her own. I couldn't even imagine taking that away from her.

I took a couple of beers from the fridge and handed one

to her as I settled next to her. She whispered thanks and took a quick swig.

"I will never stop you from working. Or not working. It's always your decision." I felt her turn toward me, but I couldn't take my eyes off the city skyline. It represented everything to me. My favorite memories after I came here were of accompanying my uncle to Manhattan for some of his client visits.. I would linger outside his office, watching men and women in suits rush past with purpose. It was invigorating. I knew I would grow up to be one of these successful New Yorkers. So, when I had to register my company, it was an easy decision to base it out of New York City rather than the west coast. Sure, the technology experts cost more here than Silicon Valley, but I had never regretted setting roots here. To deny someone else this dream would be blasphemous.

I took my fill of the beautiful skyline scene before turning to meet her gaze. She was quiet. Too quiet. The breeze picked up enough to push wild strands of her messy bun onto her face. I pushed them gently behind her ear and she almost flinched. I caressed her lovely cheekbones. In that tender moment, she leaned into my palm. A single tear dropped in my palm and I froze. I pulled her closer to me, her head nestled in the crook of my arm. I circled my arm around her, and pressed her close to me, hoping I could take away the pain that caused the tear. She shook in my embrace - her cry was muted, but a dam of tears was let loose. I shushed her, softly rubbing her back, hoping to reach a part of her deep within that would ease the hurt. My breath a whisper, I rested my cheek on her head. I realized she needed to vent this out. I found myself thinking back on my first impression of her business - that she had it easy.

She hid the hurt from everyone, while giving herself freely to anyone in need.

It felt like hours before she calmed down, her body softer and more relaxed in my arms. She sniffed, rubbing away the remnants of the tears on her face but she didn't leave my arms. I was happy to be her arm pillow.

"I am sorry. I ruined your shirt." Her voice was small and muffled.

"Not my problem. It's your hoodie." Her shoulder shook faintly and this time, it was laughter. My heart felt a thousand times lighter. I had no idea I was drowning in her tears. I lightly kissed the top of her head and she snuggled closer. It was getting colder but having her so close to me made me the warmest I had felt in years.

My phone suddenly rang in the living room and we both turned in the direction of the sound. "Must be Ryan," I mumbled, reluctant to leave her.

She finally moved, brushing her hair away. She adjusted the blanket around her.

"Go ahead. You should take it." I nodded and stood up to move when I felt her hand on my wrist, stopping me in my tracks. "This place is our secret. Don't tell him about it." I nodded. I wondered if she realized how this place had become *our* secret. I liked the sound of it.

THE CALL with Ryan was tense. He started by hurling a string of expletives at me for not picking up his calls. Eventually he settled down enough to allow me to tell the story.

"Are you serious about this arranged marriage stuff?" His voice was part curious and part incredulous. I wanted to tell him it was more than that, that I was in love with her, but not before I told Nisha. I owe it to her to tell her first.

"She hasn't agreed yet. So...we will see where it goes." There was silence on the other end. If Ryan was not shooting his mouth off, then something must be seriously wrong. "What's the matter?"

"Well, that guy you hit today...what's his name-"

"Nikhil"

"Yes. Yes, that Nikhil guy filed a complaint against you with the cops. But, then he withdrew it within a couple of hours." I had expected this from Nikhil, but it still didn't stop the chill curling in my stomach. My mother would have been ashamed of me.

"Why did he withdraw the complaint?" I rubbed the back of my neck, tracing the smooth skin of a scar I had gotten in a fight back in India.

"No idea, but that's not the problem. Gus is back again. Somehow, he got a whiff of the police complaint and has been calling the office incessantly." I swore softly. Media attention on this was bad, and Gus reporting it would be a total disaster. I heard Nisha's soft footsteps behind me and watched her enter her bedroom. "We are freezing him out so far." Hand on my hip, I stared at the polished oak floor in the kitchen and sighed. This would be bad publicity for Nisha too.

"Talk to him and tell him that it was a misunderstanding that has been resolved. Give a statement and then freeze him out." Media was a necessary evil. Better to give them information than let them interpret it on their own.

"Got it. Where are you now?"

"With Nisha." I hoped he wouldn't ask the location. I would hate lying to him.

"OK Romeo! Have fun. See you in the office tomorrow."

· · ·

I STOOD at the threshold of her bedroom, watching her tidy up the bed. She was bent over and her soft hair hung loose on one side, a dark curtain caressing her face. She tucked in the bed sheet tight and pulled up the blankets. I leaned against the door, content to watch her. Here she was not the stiff, formal executive that the world saw. She was soft, vulnerable and extremely beautiful. She smiled softly when she saw me waiting. She pulled open the drawer attached to the bed. I rushed to help her pull out the thick blanket and pillow.

"The couch is a sofa bed. I will pull it out for you."

"I am not sleepy yet." I said, as I watched her settle on the bed. Having positioned her pillow behind her, and blanket up to her waist, she patted on the empty space next to her.

"Are you sure?" I inclined my head slightly wondering what she was up to.

"You don't trust yourself, Mr. Shetty?" There was sweet challenge in her honey-dripped voice. I shook my head, clearing my head of the vivid image of me tasting her lips. I climbed on her bed, one knee in front of the other until I reached the end of the bed, next to her. I mimicked her position and sighed.

"What?" She asked, her head angled upwards to meet my eyes.

"This is not how I imagined our first time in bed," I said pointing to the Note Nirvana logo on the hoodie. She snickered.

"You can take it off if you want. You might get hot at night anyway." I removed it without hesitation. I couldn't imagine keeping it on the whole night. "What did you imagine anyway?" She snuck a glance at me, turning back to focus on tracing the design on the blanket when I looked back. Awareness of her body so close to me was like charge in the air. I willed my hands not to reach out to her.

"Just this. Talking about everything and nothing." I said, pointing to the space between us.

She pulled up her knees under the blanket and put her arms around it. Her chin resting lightly on her knees, she turned to look at me.

"I like that," she said. My lips turned up, the unspoken promise her voice held was enough to sail my heart through the night. "Do you think you would have preferred it if we were not business rivals? It would have been so much easier."

I slid down a bit, settling in to a comfortable position. My back felt relaxed, and the cool sheets felt wonderful against my skin. I pulled the blanket up to my bare chest as I pondered her question. "Not really. If you were any less accomplished, I wouldn't have respected you as much as I do now," I said. The answer came to me easily. She feigned surprise and chided me.

"Are you saying other, less accomplished women are unworthy of Mr. Arav Shetty?" I laughed, the mattress shaking lightly, moving her softly with it.

"No. But I like knowing that you understand the passion I have for my work. You put the same passion into your company." She fell back onto her pillow, lying next to me. I traced goosebumps on her arm with my eyes as her arm touched mine. She cleared her throat and stared at the ceiling.

"Do you put in the same passion in everything you do, Mr. Shetty?" I swear my heart skittered a little. As my hand found a way to hers, I somehow managed to keep it beating inside my body. I squeezed her hand lightly.

"I give my best in everything I do, Ms. Jain." She swallowed, holding my hand as tightly as I held hers. We didn't dare to look at each other. One small move too far, and I knew I wouldn't be able to stop myself. And yet, I didn't want our first time to be this way. I wanted to know her heart was mine - that she felt the same love I had for her. She had yet to choose me and damn it if I couldn't wait until she did. She broke free of my hand and turned to the other side. She tucked her arms under her head, and I heard her soft yawn. Relieved, I took it as my cue to leave. I had just begun to move off the bed when she spoke.

"Would it too much to ask..." she pulled up the blanket to her neck and said, "for you to stay and just...hold me?" I froze. I looked at her small body, completely covered in the blanket except for her head. Her hair spread out behind her, onto my pillow. Her eyes were shut tight, face pinched. I looked at my bare chest and uttered a quick prayer before sliding in the blanket without a sound. After all, I was just a man. I would need all the help I could get to endure this temptation. Or, so I thought.

The moment I touched her, I knew I didn't need to worry. As my hands slid through her slender waist, on to her hands, and my body curved against her, she relaxed in my arms. There were no bunched-up nerves or shudders. She just melded into me like water. She trusted me to keep her safe. She trusted me to shield her from the harshness of reality in this hideout of hers. I pulled her closer, her warmth filling my chest. Her chest rose and fell in rhythm with mine. I felt calm, as if everything was finally right with the world. Nisha, in my arms, made everything right.

12

NISHA

It wasn't too soon, I told myself as I drove to work. *Too soon.* I muttered as my limbs ached, rebelling against the movement to pick up my coffee. The weekend ended too soon. First with Saturday's excitement at Priya's wedding and then, yesterday dancing non-stop at her reception. Thank God Nikhil was nowhere to be seen at the reception party. I was in no mood for a replay. Arav wasn't at the reception party. This time I would have punched Nikhil myself.

I marveled at how quickly things had unraveled at the wedding, and then how they had come together at my place. I let the heat of the coffee calm the goosebumps on my arms. Waking up to find myself in Arav's arms was startling, and yet my heart felt like it would burst with happiness. Tucked in by his side, with his strong arms around me, I had felt treasured. The morning with him at my cottage was as beautiful as the bright sun outside. We made breakfast together, - bacon and eggs - and I tried my best not to stare at his bare chest. He claimed it was too hot to put the hoodie back on again, but his mischief was plain to see. He kept grinning whenever he would catch me ogling. This did lead to some scraps of bacon flying around the kitchen. All but one missed the mark.

Before he left, he asked me on an "official" date for later that day, and I found myself agreeing to it. I eyed the dress I chose for the occasion on the passenger seat and my heart raced. I was glad Arav was not around to catch me blushing at the mere thought of going on a date with him.

I made sure I wasn't smiling like a fool as I walked to my office. Enough people had remarked that I was glowing at the reception the day before. I hoped my tan make-up hid the supposed glow enough to make me look normal. I had an important decision to make that day – one that had been on my mind since the moment Arav had defended me on Saturday.

I paused at the product release countdown board, its many colored Post-it notes telling me what progress had been made. I smiled, pride overwhelming me. My team worked so hard every day, and I owed my success to them. That was why this decision was not just mine. It was something that would impact each and every one of my employees. I moved past the board; past the scores of empty chairs and desks. People were filing in slowly. I liked the quiet at this time of day. I was usually the first to arrive, coffee in hand. The calm helped me set the pace of my day, and to take control so that everything went the way I wanted it to.

As soon as I reached my desk, I pulled out my laptop and started my research. I wanted to know everything there was to know about mergers and acquisitions. I had just finished emailing both my lawyer and my CFO when my desk phone rang.

"Who?" I was sure I didn't hear Drew right the first time.

"Nikhil," he repeated. I looked at the time on my desk

clock. It was 10:30 AM. I had lost track of time and spent over three hours researching. But what was Nikhil doing here – especially at this early hour? I swallowed, panic clawing its way in.

"Send him in," I said, reaching for the bottle of water on my desk. I suddenly felt parched. I took a deep breath as I waited for him to arrive. I swallowed down a shocked gasp as Nikhil entered the office. He had stitches on the side of and under his nose, and his face was bruised. It would have been easier not to have seen him like that - to hold on to my earlier resentment of him and behavior at the wedding. Guilt seeped into my thoughts, and I found myself looking for words to amend our rift.

I stood up as he walked towards me slowly, a smug smile of victory on his face. I recognized that unwelcome smile, the gloat he often displayed when he pulled an unfortunate trick on an unsuspecting victim. It was then I realized there was only one purpose for this meeting, and that was to hurt me some more. Any trace of sympathy I had for him disappeared. I was surprised that I missed having Arav around - not to defend me, but to watch me as I faced Nikhil, unfettered by the nerves that had always gripped me before. He took a seat, his right ankle resting on his left knee. His smile grew, the stitches spreading slightly.

"Morning, darling," he said, his eyes not meaning the niceties he just uttered. I crossed my hands. Silence was my friend - I didn't deem it necessary to reply. "Are you still upset with me?" He raised his eyebrows in surprise, and I marveled at his acting abilities. All of those high-paying modeling contracts were helping him improve his skills. "Come on, I was jealous that that jerk's hands were on you."

"Careful, Nikhil. Your nose is still not healed, and I don't want to make it worse." Color rose on his face and he stood abruptly, upturning the chair behind him.

"Careful how you talk to your fiancé, Nisha. This tone won't work once we are married." His menacing voice should have struck fear in me, but I only stood taller.

"I am not your fiancé anymore. We broke up months ago, and it would be good for you to remember that."

"Oh, you and your tantrums." He touched the tender side of his face gently as if remembering a *tantrum* of mine. He shook his head, a patronizing look on his perfect face. "You know I forgive you, and I will take you back whenever you are ready. Here, take this."

I watched as he pulled out a magazine that was poking out from his pant side pocket. When I didn't make a move, he grabbed my hand and pushed the magazine into my hand. It was the latest issue of Startup INC. "I have book-marked a page for you to read." I looked down to open the magazine. I could hear the glee in his voice as he said, "You are lucky I love you so much. After that drama at Priya's wedding, no man would take you as a bride." I looked up, loathing every word he uttered. But his smile only grew. He pointed to the magazine and said, "Read. I am not going anywhere."

I began reading. It was the magazine's gossip page, which was filled with bite-sized stories from various star-tups. My eyes finally stopped at a headline that read "How Far Would You Go to Save your Company?" The reporter was Gus Reeves.

How far Would You Go to Save your Company?

WHILE MOST OF us would attend a fine wedding to support and honor the happy couple, there are those who prefer to make such an occasion all about themselves. Grapevine has it that *the* most eligible billionaire bachelor, Arav Shetty, was seen throwing a few punches at some poor guy – all in defense of his date. And, who was his date? Why, none other than Nisha Jain, CEO of Note Nirvana. Considering their companies are arch-rivals in the productivity app field, this is a huge deal. But what makes this the stuff of reality TV is that, just a few weeks ago, Arav Shetty himself swore to yours truly that he would make Nisha Jain sign her company over to him willingly. This was right after he stormed out of his meeting with her at a coffee shop. Whether he said it out of a wounded CEO's pride or because of a lover's spat remains to be seen. But how far would you go to save *your* company? Would you romance your arch-rival just to stave off a blistering attack? Would you *marry* your rival to protect your business? Arav Shetty definitely seems to be weighing these options. And while he figures it out, we cannot get enough of the evolving drama. Stay tuned!

I STARED at the article until my eyes burned. I couldn't, wouldn't look at the Nikhil's gloating face. Was this true? Was Arav really using me to save his company? I knew Gus Reeves. I had him banned from covering anything about my company, because I hated the unethical methods he used to gain information, but he did report real news, regardless of how he got it.

My heart sped, rage crushing me from inside. If this was true, then everything Arav was doing was to just a means of ensuring that his company has one less rival. All the tender words, the understanding, the care that I thought I saw in those mesmerizing eyes - was it all a lie? God - this hit the stands today, which meant EVERYONE in my world must have read it.

"I know it hurts. This is what happens when you date men who treat their women like dirt." It was hard to watch Nikhil delight in this disaster. He professed his love to me and yet, he was happy to see me crushed. Why did I ever think anything good of him? Why was he still allowed in my life?

"Get out!" He looked startled. He stood up, towering over me. In the past I would have taken a step back. But today, my hands itched to punch him in the nose again. "What?" I said at his surprised expression. "Did you expect me to run back into your arms?"

"At least you could be grateful for still having a fiancé." Only after my hand connected with his face did I realized I had slapped him. I only saw red. His sense of entitlement finally breached my last line of defense. For a moment he looked at me, stunned. I marched to the door and opened it.

"Out. Right now." He strode out of the office and I slammed the door behind him. The tingle in my palm reminded me of what I had done, but I felt no shame. That slap was for all the times he had insulted my intelligence and made me feel small. He cherished the moments I depended on him, because they made him feel good. And I had allowed it. I had allowed him to gloat while *my* work, *my* strengths were ridiculed. I took a deep, cleansing breath, and pushed the ugly memories of him out with it. My eyes landed on the magazine on the floor and my heart broke all over again. I picked it up gingerly and read it all over again.

Arav. Shame. That's what I felt. Shame at allowing myself to be used again. I seethed with resentment. I thought I finally found someone who understood my struggles, who understood me. What a fine actor he turned out to be.

My hands shook as I punched Arav's number on my phone. One ring. Two.

"Hey, miss me already?" The sounds of honking in the background was jarring. I felt hot, small beads of sweat on my forehead as I focused on breathing even. His voice, despite the rage I felt, was still as charming as it was the first day I met him.

"So, in this grand plan of yours, how did you imagine me signing over my company to you? In the throes of passion? Or when we returned from our honeymoon?" His silence felt cold and heartless. I imagined the shock on his face. He probably didn't experience the feeling of getting caught very often.

"What happened?" The calmness in his voice riled me.

"What happened? What happened? You tell me, Arav. How are you going to save your company now that I know of your disgusting plan?"

"I have no idea what you are talking about." I heard the sincerity in his voice. The voice that he had used on me since day one. Despite knowing everything about him, my heart still wanted to cave. It still wanted to believe him.

"Well page three of Startup INC. will enlighten you then." I hung up. The need to scream was building up within me. I threw the phone at the wall. It landed with an unsatisfying dull thud - I craved the cacophony of crashing noise. The phone, still sadly intact, began to ring. I knew the ringtone. Arav was trying to reach me. I wanted to stomp on the phone, to shut it off forever. Instead, I walked around my desk to my chair and sat down. The phone rang and rang. I sat there, staring at it in disgust.

Once again, I had trusted the wrong man. Once again, I wanted to believe in love, and couldn't. My eyes burned, and I blinked. My heart was breaking so forcefully that I was surprised no one could hear it. The shards of the broken pieces were cutting me up from the inside. I don't know how long I sat there, bemoaning my utter failure with men.

The door of my office flew open. I stood abruptly as I saw Arav's tall frame blocking the door from the peeping employees outside. Face drawn, his eyes raged just as much as mine.

"Move." He turned slightly to let Drew in, but his eyes never left mine. Bunched in his hands was a crushed copy of the Startup INC.

"I tried to stop-"

"Give us a moment here, Drew." I kept my gaze on Arav as Drew left the room, muttering soft obscenities at him. Arav's hands crushed the magazine further. He strode in and threw it on the desk.

"You chose to believe this?" Hands tucked in his trouser pockets, he stood a few inches away from my desk. There was a dead calmness to his voice. I crossed my hands across my chest, my own breathing uneven.

"I really made an impression on you the first time. An impression of how naive and stupid I am. Is that why you thought you could dupe me this way?" Something flickered in his eyes, a storm I had not seen before.

"You are not stupid or naive, Nisha. You are smart, hard-working and will do-"

"Stop it. Enough of all the lies." I could no longer listen to the sudden softness, the fake worry that had gotten to me before. Not this time. Not any longer.

"This article is a lie." He pointed to the crumpled magazine between us. "Every word there was twisted, and the timeline is all wrong."

"But the words were said. By you. How you will *make* me hand over my company to you." Fresh anger boiled up in me and I dropped my hands to my side in fists. He stood straighter, a deep breath as if readying himself for the *tantrums* Nikhil told me I threw.

"What do you want, Nisha?"

"As if that is important here. Would you have cared about what I wanted *after* you took over Note Nirvana?"

"Nisha, you are not listening to me. It's not true. You are not making sense-"

"Get out."

"Listen. I need you to just lis-"

"You *need* me only to save your company, Arav Shetty." Bitter laughter tore out of me, at the pathetic situation I had put myself in again with a man. "TechNotes. Didn't you tell me once that your company is your biggest savior? The one that proves to the world the kind of man you are?" I bend forward, my hands on the desk. I was sure my face looked as bitter as I felt in my heart. "I will make sure TechNotes burns to ashes. And then, you will know exactly how it feels to be crushed by someone you love." The meaning of my words hit both of us at the same time. He took a step back. His mask of anger was replaced by a tenderness I had not seen before.

"Nisha, I l-"

"I didn't mean that." I said, too quickly, my voice harsher than I intended. He flinched. "I cannot *love* someone like you, someone who is quite okay with scheming a marriage - for business. Yes, I probably might have come to care a little about you, but love..." I laughed, the bitterness clinging to every little sound I made, "...you ensured I would never expose myself to another man ever again."

He looked crushed – the kind of defeated sadness that makes you want to hug someone tight to take the hurt away. I hated myself to even feel a pinch of sympathy for him. Hands at his sides, he gazed at me, forehead creased and lips pressed. A sudden stream of sunlight lit up the room as the dark clouds outside parted. He looked glorious even in pain, and I knew his face at that moment would haunt me for a long time. Any joy I might have felt in destroying his company was forever lost.

HOURS AFTER HE LEFT, I stood up, gathering as much energy I could. I felt dead inside, but I had to do what I had to do. I strode out of the room, ensuring I didn't look sluggish when I knocked on Calista's office door. I walked in to find her hunched over her laptop with a couple others from her team. Everyone straightened up, tentative smiles on their faces. They must have heard every word uttered in the room earlier. My humiliation was out there for all to see. I hated the sympathy in Calista's eyes. I steeled my heart before it caused me to crumble right there in self-pity.

"When is our next product release?"

"A month from now. We are testing now and-"

"Two weeks. Release it to the press. And make sure that each and every subscriber refers at least three others. Float a hard-to-put-down referral scheme tomorrow especially for people coming from TechNotes. By the time we release our new features in 2 weeks, TechNotes' subscriber base should be cut in half."

"But-"

"Your bonus gets doubled if you can pull this off. Or, the company just closes in a few months if you don't."

I marched off, leaving their shocked faces behind me. I let my words hang there. All they saw right now was their CEO, enraged and fighting our arch rival, and promising destruction. I hoped that would propel them to action.

I packed my bag, my desire to work long gone. I walked out of the office and stepped out into the bustling crowd on the sidewalk. Pedestrians were rushing to escape the torrential downpour that had begun hours ago. I was in no rush. In fact, I had no idea which way I wanted to turn. I was drenched in no time, my hair plastered to my face while the freezing water numbed my body to any pain. But the numbness didn't reach inside to my aching heart. I rubbed the left side of my chest, trying to soothe the blinding pain of betrayal and sadness. I felt relief as I let the first tears fall. Here, I could cry and no one would notice. No one could tell the difference between rain and tears on this busy street. Here, I could finally embrace loneliness once again.

"Arav"

I stared at the 15-second banner on the Times Square electronic billboard. It cost millions of dollars and months of time to get that slot. The first time I saw a TechNotes ad light up the billboard, I threw an unlimited company cocktail party in celebration. Today, I wanted to smash that offensive, flashy neon billboard. It all just felt so wrong without Nisha.

"Arav" The grating voice of my attorney was insistent.

"Yes" I snapped.

"The papers are ready." The words stilled my heart for a second. But they beat faster as the TechNotes ad bloomed onto the billboard again. It felt like a sign. I felt relieved and excited. I breathed out a sigh before turning to face the sharply dressed, portly company attorney.

"Thanks, Stewart." I took the papers from him and was leafing through them when Ryan barged in.

"Note Nirvana is about to be crushed!" His face was flushed with excitement. He looked slightly haggard with his loose tie and rolled up sleeves. My heart skittered to a stop at those words.

In a moment of utter despair after Nisha's fierce condemnation, I had emailed Ryan to look after the company while I stayed away to clear my head. I had warned him of Note Nirvana's impending surprise, but I obviously wasn't clear enough about my intentions. Ryan took it as an invitation to launch a war.

"I told you they were looking for funds, right? Actually, I was wrong." Hands on his hips, his victorious smugness was nauseating. "Nisha is begging for money everywhere. The company has been growing so quickly that they are running out of money, fast. There have been multiple rounds of investor funding discussions. And guess who was almost ready to sign the dotted line?" I angled my head, not trusting my voice to be polite to him. "Steve Williams."

He clapped my back, grinning from ear to ear. Steve was the smartest guy in our neighborhood high school, and no one was surprised when he was accepted into Harvard. Today, he ran one of the largest start-up investment groups in Silicon Valley. If Nisha convinced him to invest, it was a pretty impressive feat.

"You said he *was* interested. Not anymore?" My voice betrayed the rage I felt for what I suspected Ryan would say next.

"Bingo! I called in a favor and he agreed. Note Nirvana will be crushed in a couple of months! We win bro! We win."

Fists in the air, he made it sound like we just won the Powerball lottery. In another time and world, I would have joined him, and taken immense pleasure in seeing our competitor sink. Not today. Today, my heart ached for Nisha, for the unfairness of all this, even though it was quite common in the cutthroat world of business.

"What's the matter?" He sobered, finally noticing I wasn't joining him in the celebration. The presence of Steve in the room got me a suspicious look from Ryan. "Is everything okay?"

"Steve, can you please give us a moment?"

Shaking his head, Steve exited the room, leaving just Ryan and I alone. He leaned on my desk, hands crossed, with a look of trepidation.

"You screwed up, didn't you?" His look of accusation did nothing to me. My heart was too buried in pain to feel the sting of my best friend's disappointment. I told him about the article that was published and the showdown that led to her to declaring war against TechNotes.

"So, what! Who cares? It's not like you're in love with her. You're surrounded by women who would die just to be your one-night-stand!" said Ryan. I shoved the papers into his hand.

"I am not interested in any of that," I said through gritted teeth. I really didn't want to make this worse. I watched him read through the papers, shock on his face.

"What the -"

"I was planning to let you know after Steve left," I said. He slammed the papers on the desk.

"*This...is...not...fair*," he said, punctuating each word with a tap of his finger on the desk. "You know what? This is worse than unfair. This is a total betrayal." I couldn't tell if he was more enraged, or more devastated. "you know what? I can't do this with you. I'm out." He stormed out of the room.

The bang of the door reverberated in my empty office. I sighed, trying to rub my incessant, three-day-long headache away. Ryan was just one of many who would be upset by this decision. Not that I cared. I knew this was the right thing to do. I did not build a multi-billion-dollar company by making bad decisions, and this decision would be the best one yet.

"You've got to be kidding me." I muttered under my breath as I watched maintenance men in hard hats closing off the elevator area. The security guard of the building was busy sticking a repair note on the wall next to the elevator. Apparently, it would be out for the next thirty minutes. *Great. Just great.* I strode towards the stairwell, bumping into other people who were braving the stairs. Excusing myself repeatedly, I took two steps at a time, wishing I was already in Nisha's office.

Her office didn't hold good memories anymore, not after the disastrous confrontation I had with her the last time. Hurtful words were thrown around like confetti, and we parted promising to destroy each other. I regretted it all now. In the space of three days, I had realized anger was a heavy burden to carry. I couldn't keep giving in to my worst nature and still hope to build a relationship.

I pushed through the heavy metal door of her floor into the crisp air conditioning. My heart sped up as I found myself striding behind another employee who was heading in. Drew was not at the front desk. Not that I was going to wait for him to check with Nisha. If my past experience with him was any indicator, he would murder me with his desk phone just to block me from getting to her office. I passed through the golden mandalas on the screen towards Nisha's office.

"Arav? Hey." I recognized that voice. I looked back to find Drew pacing towards me. *Not today bro.*

I picked up my pace, taking advantage of the head start I got. When I looked back, Drew was already on the phone calling security. I rolled my eyes at his antics. Getting me arrested was probably his favorite fantasy. "Arav. Stop running around. Wait–" I saw two security guards behind him already. I quickened. People were peeking out of conference rooms at the commotion. But I wasn't far from her office even though the security guards had gained ground impressively in the last few seconds. I chanced a look back only to find one of them at just an arm's length away. I should have panicked but I was almost there. I barged in to her office.

"Nisha we need to ta-" I stopped, stunned to find the room empty. I turned back but promptly bumped in to the security guard. Drew followed behind and stood panting. I turned back to look at her empty desk. It looked too clean, too organized and I wondered if she was even in the building today.

"This is why I was trying to stop you. She's not here." He was bent over, panting.

"Then why did you call security?" I asked. He looked back, waving a hand at them to leave.

"Force of habit when you're around." He straightened up, smoothing his tie. "Don't roll your eyes. You keep forcing your way in here." I nodded and looked back.

"Where is she?" I asked. His gaze moved to her desk, worry creasing his forehead.

"We don't know. She hasn't come to work since that day you...in the last three days." There was no bite in his voice.

"She's working from home?" I was confused. What did

he mean? He shook his head, and for the first time, his eyes met mine and I could see he was scared.

"We haven't heard from her since that day. No one has. Her calls go to voicemail, and now even that is full." My heart raced. Panic seized me, and I felt as if something heavy was pressing on my chest. "Have *you* tried calling her?" Drew asked. His voice was small, but hopeful. Unfortunately, like an idiot, I hadn't called because I was so busy licking my wounds. I shook my head. "OK." His voice shook a little. I rubbed my chest, trying to ease the tightness I felt. *God, where are you Nisha?* I fished out my phone to call her, when it flashed with Kamlesh Jain's number. Nisha's father was calling me. I picked it up immediately.

"Has Nisha been in touch with you?" His deathly calm voice was unnerving. I rubbed my neck, dispelling some of the tension. This meant no one had heard from her yet.

"No, sir. I am in her office right now. I had no idea she hadn't been in touch with anyone." After a moment of silence, during which horrible images of what could have happened to her flickered through my mind, he spoke.

"I thought you guys were getting along rather well?" I sighed, a well of sadness crushing me. No matter how hard I tried to deny it, I did hurt her enough for her to do this. I thought about telling him that, but decided there was no point.

"We did. I got busy with some work stuff and we were not in touch." Drew shook his head in disapproval. I turned my back on him. I didn't need more reminders of that day. "Did you file a police report?"

"I am on my way to the police station now. It's not unusual for her to spend the night at her office. But she didn't come home yesterday either, and we received no word from her, so her grandmother got suspicious. Her staff thought she might be working from home. So, we all only realized she was really missing this morning." I cursed under my breath. Two days already. I began pacing the room.

My mind went to kidnapping. Just contemplating the possibility made me see red. The kidnapper would have a lot to gain. Kamlesh Jain's gruff voice snapped me out of my disturbing chain of thoughts. "I called everyone in her circle. No one has heard from her. It's almost as if she vanished off the face of the earth. As if she doesn't want to be found."

Thunder blasted outside, and thick droplets of rain splatted noisily on glass of her office windows. Of course. She probably didn't want to be found. And there was one place where she could hide from the world, without anyone knowing where to find her. Anyone but me. I gripped the phone tight, my breath picking up. She had to be there, or else I would truly be lost. Still on the phone with Kamlesh, I sprinted out of her office towards the stairs.

"I think I may have an idea where she is. I will call you in an hour, sir." I hung up and charged down the stairs. I was panting by the time I reached my car, but I couldn't relax until I found her, safe in her cottage in Englewood Cliffs.

14

ARAV

Leaves swatted at my car as I drove through the winding lanes to Nisha's cottage. Water gushed through the sloping terrain, while the trees swayed ominously above me. The rain gods were in no mood for mercy. I was at least glad I was not stuck in New York traffic. I would probably have sprinted through the streets like a madman to get to Nisha. I prayed to all thirty million and three gods that Nisha was safe and warm in her cottage, rather than a victim of the other horrible circumstances my mind kept conjuring up. My phone buzzed. It was Ryan again, and I let it go to voicemail. He would know what was on my mind now, without a doubt. The phone rang again, the incessant noise driving me crazy. I pushed the speaker button on my car.

"What?" I barked.

"Are you really doing it?" His voice was quiet and had the clear ring of an ultimatum.

"Yes" I sounded clipped and I didn't care. He didn't answer for a moment and I checked my car dashboard to make sure we were still connected. A thunder cracked loud enough for our cell connection to cackle.

"You really love her, don't you?" I gripped the steering wheel. Right now, I would die for her if that was what it took to keep her safe.

"Doesn't matter. She hates me now."

"I'll talk to her. She needs to know the truth." I bet she did but where was she?

"Listen, I will talk to you later."

"Ok. Arav...I am sorry, man. I shouldn't have-"

"It's okay. I get it. We will talk later." I cut off the call as I neared her cottage. I sighed with relief when I saw her Audi parked on the side.

I parked my car next to hers and grabbed the papers from the front seat, tucking them under my suit jacket. I slammed the car door as I rushed to her front porch, already drenched from the pouring rain. I stood in front of her door, looking frantically for the doorbell. All I found was the hidden keypad, which was useless to me. She never built this cottage for visitors, after all. Warm light shone from inside. I was sure she was in there. I banged on the door, but the roaring river drowned out the sound. The strong winds that blew felt particularly threatening amidst the trees. Fallen brown leaves whipped in the air. I dug my hands in my coat pockets, wondering if the chill I felt down to the bone was due to the rain, or just the void that Nisha had left within me. I knocked again, dread starting to slip into my heart. What if she *wasn't* there? Where else would she go? And who *was* in there? I had just raised my hand to knock again when the door opened.

Nisha yelped as big, cold drops of water dripping from my coat hit her face. I felt my heart stammer to a slow beat as I watched her wipe her face with her arm. She had her hair tied up in a severe bun, and she stood barefoot in grey pajama pants and a Note Nirvana hoodie. Was it the same hoodie that she had lent me when I was here? She crossed her hands, hiding the company logo. I looked up, meeting her slightly swollen eyes. She had been crying, and it broke my heart that I was the cause of it. I would deal with that later, but first, I had to do something more important. I fished my phone from my suit pocket and handed it to her.

"Call your dad now. He is worried sick." She looked up from my phone in surprise. She took it from me and dialed his number.

"No, this is Nisha. I am fine, Dad. What were you worried about?" Her father's annoyed voice crackled through the phone, though I couldn't make out any of his words. "I am okay, Dad. I am really okay." She turned away from me as she held the phone with both her hands. "No...it's not him...No, please he is not to blame. Please promise me you won't harass him?" There was silence on her end and she added, "Yes, he found me after all. So, keep your promise Dad. Okay?" She nodded and said goodbye.

Wind whipped my coat again as I stood waiting at the front door. With a deep sigh, she turned around, her face aging in those few minutes. I swallowed, guilt tearing at my heart once again. The wind howled, and it sounded so much like the pain in my heart. She handed my phone back and stood holding the door. Droplets of rain fell inside her house, kissing her bare feet.

"Can I step in for a bit?" She nodded too quickly, and I stepped in without wasting a second. The loud wind was finally muted as she shut the door, and the house was drenched in silence. I shrugged out of my wet coat as I looked around. Pizza boxes sat open in the kitchen, while the living room was littered with tissues and chocolate wrappers. I looked back at the bedroom. The last time I was there, I had promised her an eternity of happiness without uttering a word. I felt my face heat up and when I looked back at Nisha, I knew she was recalling the same thing. It was time. I took a deep breath and pried the papers from my suit jacket, where I had hidden them to keep them dry.

"Read this." I demanded as I handed it to her. She looked back and forth between me and the papers, then took them silently. I watched as she smoothed the them and started reading. Her forehead creased as she went through the first lines of the document, looking up often at me in confusion. In just a few seconds, her head whipped up in shock. Her mouth made a perfect O as realization of the meaning of those papers dawned on her. Her head moved furtively as her eyes tried to catching up with the words she was reading. She looked up midway, her eyes flashing anger.

"Is this a joke?"

"No."

"Get out." She shoved the papers at me and opened the front door again. Cold wind roared, slapping us with punishing drops of chilled water as I tucked the papers in my pocket. Without my coat, the rain felt like ice. Her chest was heaving, and her eyes shone with angry tears. I pushed the door to close it, but she held on tightly to the door handle and it refused to budge. I pushed again, and she held on, stubborn as a mule. I stood with my hands on my hips, watching her hair whip her face in the wind. She was already getting drenched, but she didn't move an inch. I dropped my head in defeat. She left me with no choice.

"You asked for it" She looked up, startled as I picked her up. The unexpected action tore a yelp from her, and she released the door. I pushed the door closed with my foot and moved towards the bedroom. She kicked her legs in the air, struggling to get down, but she was hardly a match for my determination. All I needed was for her to listen. I plunked her down on the bed, and she immediately sat straight up. She tried getting up, but I placed my hands on her shoulders and pushed her down to sit at the edge of the bed. She tried getting up again, and I pinned her down into a sitting position with my hands. When she tried pushing my arms away, I grabbed her wrists and held them tightly, but gently while I kneeled in front of her. Her struggling softened as she realized I was actually on my knees, pleading with her to listen to me. I rested our hands on her lap though I still had held her wrists tight.

"Just hear me out, just once." Her chin wobbled, and she sniffed. She looked away, still defiant. I released an exaggerated sigh. "Fine. Don't look at me." A sigh escaped me. "Those papers are not a joke."

"TechNotes is your life's work!" Her glare was a challenge.

"It absolutely is. And I am giving it to you now." I loosened my grip slowly, testing whether she would run. When she didn't make any sudden movements, I pulled the document out of my pocket and tucked it back in her hands. "You were right all along. We cannot love each other because we are too much in love with our companies. We cannot sustain a marriage if we are always conspiring against each other's first love. One of us has to make a sacrifice."

Tears streamed down her face on to her hands, making tiny splashes. I stared at the little drops as I continued. "Well, I have decided it will be me. The journey has begun to feel lonely for some time. Did you ever attend those success celebration parties at your company where the happiness felt so fake...so hollow?" She gave a small nod as she wiped her tears with the back of her palm. She put her hand back in my hands and I reveled in that. "I have felt that more and more for the past year. But that might also be because Note Nirvana was kicking my can."

She snickered, a watery smile bringing some much-needed color on her face. "And then, I met the company founder...and I was no longer the same." My voice was a whisper as I recalled our first meeting. I looked up, meeting her soft gaze. A tinge of sadness returned in her face and I squeezed her hands gently. "Since then, Drew has called security on me three times, I punched a guy at a wedding, I almost killed my best friend because he had plans to shut your company down, and today, I got my first ever reckless driving ticket." Her eyes widened in shock as I pulled out the thoroughly wet ticket that the officer had handed over to me at Palisades Interstate Parkway.

"You, on the other hand," I said pointing at her, "you got Note Nirvana to the top of the charts single-handedly, while I was monkeying around. Clearly, I cannot be trusted with running a company anymore. I am too...emotional." She swatted at my arm as we shared a moment of silent laughter. "I am turning this company over to you, Nisha." I sobered, the decision feeling so right. "Because you are going to do great things with it. I am selling this company to you for zero dollars because that is what it's worth to me without you at my side." I straightened, cupping her face. "I am done proving myself to the world. I only care what you think about me. I love you, Nisha and I would be the luckiest man in the world if you loved me back."

Her fingers closed over the papers, the sound of crumpling the only movement between us. She swallowed, tears streaming down in revolt. She didn't even try wiping them this time.

"You do know I am going to make this official, right?" She held up the crumpled legal documents in hand.

"I wouldn't expect anything less. All you need to do is sign it," I said, hopefully, though my heart was cautious of feeling too relieved. I wiped her tears with my thumb.

"But I don't appreciate you staying at home doing nothing while I slog over managing two companies." A small smile lit up her eyes.

"I would be busy too. I think I know what I want to do next." She raised her eyebrows.

"Care to offer some details?"

"I am planning a seed investment organization for technology start-ups by women. I have met with a couple of friends who are looking to invest. Hopefully, within the next couple of months, I can share more details with you." She blinked faster, fighting more tears. She moved to kneel down on the floor, facing me. Cupping my face, she gently kissed my lips. To say I didn't want to deepen the kiss would be a lie. But I was too disoriented to move an inch. I felt her gentleness - a love intense to the bone.

"Will you marry me?" she asked, a blush coloring her cheeks just the way I loved. I traced one cheek with my fingers, feeling more complete than I had ever felt.

"I think I can arrange that."

EPILOGUE

Anshi

Three Months Later...

No. No. No! I ducked behind a couple, matching my pace with their stroll as yet another cameraman passed us. Thankfully, he was too busy admiring the hot pink lehenga I was hiding behind to notice my muted grey ensemble. The small matter of my hair dyed pitch black instead of its usual electric blue might also have had a role in keeping me obscure. Involuntarily, I smoothed my shoulder length hair, tucking it behind my ear.

Leave it to my father to have a party that had more media people invited than family and friends. I had hoped Nisha's engagement party would be a quieter affair, considering how much she hates crowds.

I looked around for a quiet spot that would give me the highest chance of not being spoken to. I found a nondescript corner at the back of the room that looked perfect. It stood right next to golden floor-to-ceiling curtains, which would allow me to easily hide if anyone approached me. I walked quietly and quickly, avoiding eye contact with a group of guests who were in animated conversation with a figure in grey suit. The figure's rather well-toned back was to me, and I carefully made my way around him as discretely as possible. The group's conversation quieted down as I passed, and I cringed. They had obviously noticed me. I definitely wasn't as stealthy as I had hoped to be. I felt their eyes on my back, but I moved fast, making my way toward my hiding spot. A lone chair awaited me in the corner, and I took a seat, sighing in relief.

Guests milled around in finery. The huge banquet hall could hold five hundred guests, and I was pretty sure the number of people in the hall at that moment matched the max limit. Not many people would want to miss Kamlesh Jain's daughter's engagement, after all.

The wine, the networking, the riches...my breath hitched as a familiar pang of suffocation gripped me. I looked around urgently for a sight that would distract me from an impending anxiety attack. My eyes landed on Nisha, my beautiful little sister. Immediately, I relaxed. She was radiant. Draped in a beautiful golden saree, her blouse slinking off her shoulders, she looked like a goddess. She was talking to a group of suited men, her arm casually draped around her fiancé, Arav. Her eyes shone with happiness, and my attention turned to Arav, the apparent source of her glow. He was handsome, I had to admit. Hands in his pockets, he was angled towards Nisha as if she was his center. I had heard of his business conquests, and of his troubled family past. Maybe Nisha centered him and helped him heal the wounds that a lot of us carry unnoticed.

I hadn't met Arav personally yet, but Nisha had told me

enough for me to understand that she had finally found a man who really *sees* her. And that was enough for me. I had seen her struggle as the youngest daughter of Kamlesh Jain; first shadowed by the enormity of our father's success, and then, by her older sisters. Sara, the eldest, was the *perfect* one, setting standards that we either couldn't or wouldn't match, and I was the *troubled* one, leaving poor Nisha no option but to be the *ignored* one. I wish I had been there to help her more, but the truth was I was too busy rebelling - too busy turning up my nose at my father.

At least she hadn't ended end up in rehab like me. Nope. Instead, she went to Yale, and now she owned not just Note Nirvana, but TechNotes too, making her one of the richest tech founders in New York City. pride welled up in my heart just thinking about it.

As if Nisha cold sense my feelings from across the room, she turned toward me, and her eyes lit up with surprise as they met mine. She excused herself from her guests and hastened to reach me. I barely had time to stand up when she crashed into me, squeezing the life out of me with a tight hug. I struggled to stand straight - she didn't seem to want to let me go. Her shoulders shook. My eyes burned with unshed tears. I felt deep down just how much I missed this girl.

"No more tears, now," I said. "No one wants to see mascara running down the bride's face." I gave her a tissue from the table. She sniffed and gave me a watery smile as she unsuccessfully tried to dab at her eyes. I took the tissue from her and wiped her face.

"I thought you wouldn't be able to make it," she said, standing still as she still let me clean up her mascara mess. I shrugged. Her chin wobbled again but she took some deep breaths and reined it in. "Did you see Dad?" I shook my head. I didn't know how to face him.

"Not yet."

"Am I interrupting?" We both turned to find Arav, his concerned eyes only for Nisha. Brows knitted, he stepped closer to her. I bit my lip to keep from smiling as I saw his protective instincts in action. I didn't want to embarrass the couple, but the exchange was so cute. Nisha settled next to him, their hands entangled. I cleared my throat.

"Um...this is Anshi," Nisha said, looking at me with as much pride as if I had just returned from the war front victorious. I reveled in the love my sister showered on me. It was a balm to my hurt pride.

"Ah, the favorite sister," said Arav, giving me a mock bow. "So, you are real. Glad to finally meet you. I was beginning to wonder if Nisha made up stories about your...ahem...adventures, just to keep me scared."

"Not sure about the stories, but if you hurt her, I will kill you." Arav gave me an approving smile, as if he expected nothing less from me.

"What is this obsession with violence in your family?" he said. Nisha laughed joyfully - a sound that would remain in my heart for a long time to come. She was truly happy. I stared at both of them, the contentment of having found each other all over their faces. For a moment, despite all the crap that was in my life, I wished...I wished for love like that. So simple and pure.

A blinding light startled us, and just like that, my thoughts were shattered. A group of photographers surrounded us, and the clicking of cameras was all around us. Nisha and Arav turned towards them as smoothly as they could manage and smiled. Not with the same bright, genuine smiles they had had a few seconds before, but public smiles that would please the page three reporters.

Panic seized me. I didn't want to be in the papers again. The last time I was on page three, my father had to send me away for three months. I managed to slip away from the glare, but I could sense someone following me. I looked back to find a reporter with a greedy smile behind me. I kept walking, picking up speed, and stopping only to step around people. A waiter passed by, and I picked up a glass full of bubbly liquid. A quick swig and the rich, delicious warmth of champagne made its way down my throat. Unfortunately, it did nothing to ease my panic.

"Anshi Jain?" I heard him call, as if to confirm that I was indeed the scandalous daughter of Kamlesh Jain. I resisted reacting to his words, but he knew! My breath came in faster, and my hands clutched the glass harder. Then, suddenly, I heard a commotion behind me. I took a quick look just in time to see a reporter crash into someone in a grey suit. The reporter looked annoyed as he tried to wipe liquid off of his clothes. I could still feel eyes boring into my back. I took a quick right, toward some tables behind the crowd, and hoped the reporter, and whoever else was following, had lost me.

I saw an empty seat a table and sat down, adjusting the skirt of my grey *lehenga*. I focused on my breathing, and on little things around me to distract myself. I looked at the tiny mirrors all over the body of my skirt and blouse. They gave sparkled under the bright lights, making the material look as if...as if it were...

"...a shimmering river under the moonlight." I looked up, startled to stare into a pair of the deepest blue eyes I had ever seen. I sucked in a breath. His eyes seemed to read my soul, but the charming smile on his lips unleashed some scandalous thoughts. For a moment, I worried he could read every one of them.

"Excuse me?" I managed to say while trying not to fan myself. I took another quick sip of the champagne. Bad idea - felt even hotter. The handsome stranger, with his perfectly-set sandy hair, let out a low laugh. I noticed the grey suit and realized he was the guy who had bumped into the reporter.

"I had been imagining what your voice might sound like since the moment I watched you slide into the shadows, as if you were someone with a reason to hide," he said. He stood standing, his hands in his pant pockets. His velvety voice embraced me in delicious warmth.

"It is better to hide me, trust me," I said, alcohol making me bolder than necessary. He angled his head, watching as I took another sip of champagne. His eyes lingered a few moments longer on my lips. I wet them nervously, feeling suddenly self-conscious. It had been a while since a man looked at me as I was something to be desired, not shunned.

"You seem like someone who should be unleashed on the world, not hidden, never hidden." I gazed back at him. His words sounded like a song to my heart.

"Who are you, again?" I asked hoarsely. A part of me cringed at the idea of baring my soul to him, but mostly, I didn't care. It felt safe, somehow. He took the chair next to me, his eyes never leaving mine.

"I'm Ryan Penn. The groom's best friend and best man . . . and your sister is going to be my new boss. I'm the CFO at Tech Notes." I stared at his extended hand as if it were a live wire that threatened to burn me.

"What was that you were saying about rivers and moonlight?" I said instead, my right hand tight around the flute of my champagne glass.

"Ah...your *lehenga.*" The hindi word rolled off his tongue

with a cute accent. He seemed unembarrassed. "Even though you look like it's caging you in, it actually suits your spirit."

"What do you know about my spirit, Mr. Penn?" His answering smirk got my anger flaring. He sat back, his left-hand index finger tracing circles on the white tablecloth.

"You are very easy to read, Ms Jain. Or, rather, your tattoos are." He traced the beginning of the tattoo on my right arm, his touch feathery. I had gotten that tattoo when I was seventeen - a tree, rotting from within, turning to ash every day. The part on my arm was the part everyone could see. No one had ever seen the end of the tattoo, sat under my blouse over my left breast.

"You love too deeply. You hurt too deeply. But you never stop. Just like the river. Only the bright moon can tell the world what a beauty you are." His warm gaze left a heat trail all over my body. I blinked, words drying up on my lips. He sat back, crossing his right ankle on his left knee. I swallowed.

"For someone who spends his day crunching numbers, you are unexpectedly good with words."

"It's easy when the scenery is so inspiring." I nodded as he had just given me a great piece of advice. He began staring at someone behind me. I looked back to find Nisha and Arav, hand in hand, spending a candid moment alone. I smiled, watching their love shine through the facade of this celebration that my father threw.

"Do you wonder if we can be as lucky as they are?" he asked. I looked back to find his gaze fixed on me, as if I held the answer to the most important question of his life.

"I don't believe that kind of love is in the cards for me." I said, the words finally defining what I had been feeling all night. The blue of his eyes darkened. I wanted to tell him he was as easy to read as I was.

He was about to say something when a stunningly beautiful woman stopped right next to him. The burgundy dress she wore clung closely to her like a second skin, showing off every inch of her voluptuous body. She bent down to kiss him right on those delicious lips, claiming him for her own. After what seemed forever, he broke the kiss. Wiping his lips with the cuff of his sleeve, he looked directly at me. His eyes had turned cold. He stood, placing his arms around the slender waist of the woman. My heart thumped hard, and disappointment was bitter on my tongue as I watched her pull him to herself and take him away. I looked away, determined that he not see the hurt on my face. After all, I just met him, and had no claim to him. I didn't notice where he went, as I refused to even look in that direction.

I sat sipping my champagne, every drop dragging me deeper into a calm state. A waiter stopped next to me, replacing my empty glass with a full one, and handing me a neatly folded napkin. "A note for you," he said. I opened the napkin, fingers slightly shaking, as I had an idea who might have sent it. The handwriting was neat, with a slight angle to the right.

"It's amazing how different the world looks when you let yourself dream. So, go ahead and dream, Ms. Jain." I looked around, my eyes searching for Ryan. I found him in a group, one hand holding a glass of amber liquid and the other in his pocket. The woman had slipped a hand around his waist, but he stood stiff. Just when the image of her draped around him began to burn my eyes, he met my gaze. He raised his glass and inclined his head slightly. I nodded - a secret, wordless promise.

Dream, he said. And so, I will.

ALSO BY SHILPA MUDIGANTI

Ryan and Anshi's story continues in...

Love by Surprise.

Serial dater. Workaholic. Math Wizard.

I've heard them all, but that's not who I am.

I'm just Ryan.

I've dated my fair share of women but it's not like I have commitment issues. I just never met a woman that I wanted to give my heart to... until I met *her*.

Anshi Jain.

She's a spiraling mess struggling to get her life back on track and I can't help being fascinated by her. She has a past that should have sent me running in the other direction, but I have no desire to let her go. Leave it to me to fall for the one woman who is too stubborn to accept my help.

https://books2read.com/u/3RayLR

AFTERWORD

Dear Reader,

Your time is precious. So, I greatly appreciate you investing it in reading my book. I hope you enjoyed it. Reader recommendations are crucial to an author's success. If you enjoyed my book, I humbly request you to please leave a review of the book here. Even if it's only a line or two, it would make a tremendous difference.

Thank you again,
*   Shilpa*

ACKNOWLEDGMENTS

As is common with every author's journey to completing a book, this story evolved in to what you read today by the contributions of many.

First, I am grateful to my parents for their love and dedication in giving me a lifestyle that gave me the opportunity and luxury to dabble in writing. I am lucky to be their child.

Second, I am thankful to my husband for his countless hours of patience with me when I am off visiting my imaginary world. He manifests his love in the quietest ways known to mankind, but I have grown to recognize and treasure them.

Third, to Melissa Keir, my publisher - From business partners to friends, you have been one of the most positive, encouraging people I have met. If I am writing to this day, you have a huge contribution in keeping me focused. I am forever grateful to that.

Fourth, to my editor, Jessica Martinez – You kept the dream alive. You made me believe in the story of Arav and Nisha. Even when you ripped it apart during your editing, you put it back together lovingly. I wouldn't have had the courage to push this baby in to the world without your keen eye and love.

Finally, to you, my reader – An author's journey is a solitary one. But she makes this journey to meet you, to hear you whisper your thoughts as you read the words plucked from her soul. I wrote this book for you. I sincerely wish the time you put in to reading this is a memorable one.

ABOUT THE AUTHOR

Shilpa Mudiganti believes life is too short to read tragedies. She writes romance and fantasy fiction that always has a happy ending. No matter how hard the circumstances are, the hero and heroine will walk into the sunset holding hands. IT professional by day and dreamer by night, she loves to hear from her readers about their life experiences. There is no inspiration like life.

Say hello to Shilpa by emailing her or drop her a private message on Instagram. (https://www.instagram.com/shilpa_mudiganti/)

If you would like to get an automatic email when Shilpa's new book is released and get FREE short stories, please sign up here. (http://bit.ly/givemebookupdates)

Shilpa is also the author of:

Lost & Found – A Valentine's Day Novella

Aisha lost the love of her life to fate. And then Liam happened. But is she ready to risk her heart again?

Always You – A Second Chance Romance Novella

What will happen when two broken people with a past come together? Can they forgive and heal?

Subway – A New York Diaries Short Story

Love is naive. Love is strange. What would you do if you fall for a stranger in a subway?

Forever Yours – A Short Story

Amelia loves Aaron, her fiancé. She also loves Damon. Can one be in love with two men at the same time? How do you define infidelity? Or fidelity?